hoo HAH!

Once again the call of the Wild Goose echoes across marshland and glade as MAD Strikes Back!

Even as you read this, giant presses are roaring and pounding, sleek black trucks are racing through the night to bring you this all-new edition of MAD reading.

Poopeye! Prince Violent! Teddy and the Pirates! —they're all included in this handy reference volume. Is it any wonder all America has acclaimed the new MAD as a veritable quagmire of ideas?

DON'T DELAY! Invest now and know the pride of owning this magnificent ½″ shelf of the World's great Literature!

Its tiny pages crammed with inscrutable type, its sturdy binding reinforced to snap shut on the thumbs of unwary browsers, the new MAD is one book you can't put down—because MAD Strikes Back!

"Distinguished companion Volume to The MAD Reader in the low-price field."

ibooks
new york
www.ibooksinc.com

DISTRIBUTED BY SIMON & SCHUSTER, INC

written by
HARVEY KURTZMAN

drawn by
JACK DAVIS
BILL ELDER
WALLACE WOOD

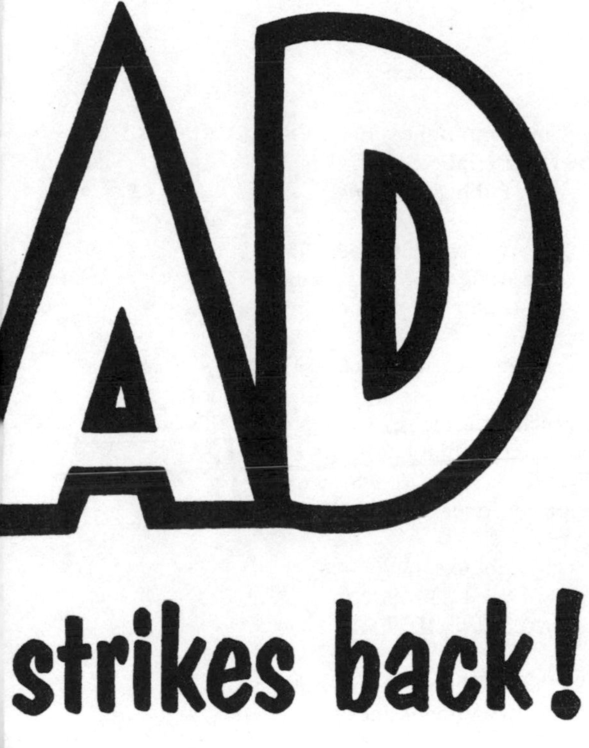

strikes back!

with a straight talk from BOB & RAY

An ibooks, inc. Book

Distributed by Simon & Schuster, Inc.
1230 Avenue of the Americas, New York, NY 10020

ibooks, inc.
24 West 25th Street
New York, NY 10010

The ibooks World Wide Web Site Address is:
http://www.ibooksinc.com

Visit www.madmag.com

ISBN 0-7434-4478-7
First ibooks, inc. printing March 2002
10 9 8 7 6 5 4 3 2 1

Printed in the U.S.A.

CONTENTS

INTRODUCTION
by Grant Geissman

The book you are holding is a facsimile reprint of *MAD Strikes Back!*, and is the second in a new series of 50th Anniversary reprints–published by ibooks–of the early *MAD* paperbacks.

The original version of *MAD Strikes Back!* (published in June 1955 by Ballantine Books) followed closely on the heels of the very successful *The MAD Reader* (also available in a facsimile edition from ibooks). It duplicated the formula of its immediate predecessor, reformatting material that originally appeared in the twenty-three-issue run of the *MAD* comic book. All of the original material was written (and laid out for the artists) by *MAD* creator Harvey Kurtzman, and features the core group of early *MAD* artists that included Bill Elder, Jack Davis, and Wallace Wood. Kurtzman and his editor at Ballantine, Bernard Shir-Cliff, selected all the material for inclusion and, like *The MAD Reader*, *MAD Strikes Back!* was a hit upon publication. Between June and December 1955, Ballantine went back to press with the book four times.

Continuing the tradition of having well-known personalities contribute introductions to the *MAD* books (Roger Price wrote the foreword for *The MAD Reader*), the popular comedy team Bob and Ray was recruited to write the introduction for *MAD Strikes Back!* Bob Elliot and Ray Goulding were then enjoying great success with their syndicated radio show, and they and *MAD* had quite a mutual admiration society going. In the wonderfully arcane fashion that was a Bob and Ray trademark, "A Straight Talk by Bob and Ray" focuses on minutia that has nothing to do with *MAD.* (The spot illustrations to the piece were done by Bill Elder and are the only new artwork to appear in this volume.) Bob and Ray later contributed a series of articles for the magazine version of *MAD.* Most of these were ghostwritten by Tom Koch, one of Bob and Ray's regular writers. Because Koch's name and address appeared on the scripts that were submitted, *MAD*'s editors contacted Koch directly, and he ended up becoming one of *MAD* Magazine's most prolific writers.

Leading off the line-up in *MAD Strikes Back!* is Kurtzman's treatment of *Prince Valiant*, "Prince Violent!," (*MAD* #13, July 1954, illustrated by Wallace Wood). Created, written, and illustrated by the legendary Hal Foster in 1930, *Prince Valiant* is one of the most successful and enduring syndicated comic strips of all time (seventy years later the strip is still being syndicated with new installments). Kurtzman strongly disapproved of violence in both comic books and comic strips, and of Prince Valiant's routine romanticism and glorification of it. Hal Foster's impeccable draftsmanship cast a long shadow of influence over cartoonists and illustrators of the day, and Wood here is clearly enjoying the opportunity to pay tribute to and poke fun at Foster. (After doing the strip for forty years, in 1970 advancing arthritis forced Hal Foster to search for a permanent replacement, and in an interesting echo of his early work in *MAD*, Wallace Wood illustrated a number of *Prince Valiant* Sunday pages before Foster finally decided upon John Cullen Murphy as his successor.)

"Captain TVideo" (*MAD* #15, September 1954, illustrated by Jack Davis) takes on *Captain Video and His Video Rangers*, which was one of the most popular (and award-winning) children's shows of the 1950s. Airing on the perpetually third-rate DuMont Network, *Captain Video* was first telecast on June 27, 1949, and ran until the collapse of the network in 1955. Said to have an expense account for props of $25 a week (!), the show was a low-budget wonder, with painted-on spaceship controls and rickety sets; many of the Ranger's "space weapons" were actually barely disguised common household objects. And in a prescient nod to the power of merchandising, premium items—such as plastic replicas of Captain Video's helmet, decoder ring, and space gun—were routinely hawked on the program. The show was telecast in black and white, and Kurtzman approximated this effect by including horizontal lines running across each panel, and by printing the story in black and white (expressly not utilizing the cheap-looking comic book color that was used in most of the stories in *MAD*'s first twenty-three issues).

The charming and clever "Puzzle Page!" feature (*MAD* #19, January 1955, rendered by Bill Elder) that appears here and there throughout this book was originally part of one consecutive story (entitled "Puzzle Pages!," under the heading "Filler Dept."), and was re-configured to suit the needs of the paperback format. "Puzzle Page!" sends up the many such one-page "fillers" that are regularly seen in vintage comic books. A somewhat related feature, "Believe It or Don't!" (*MAD* #23, May 1955, illustrated by Wallace Wood), looks at the long-running newspaper strip *Ripley's Believe It or Not.* Created and illustrated by Robert L. Ripley in the early 1920s, each installment consisted of several incredible "strange but true" facts, and proved to be an irresistible target for Kurtzman. After *MAD* graduated to the magazine format with its 24th issue in July 1955 (selling for "25¢—Cheap!"), a similar feature (entitled "Strangely Believe It!," also illustrated by Wallace Wood) was regularly contributed to the magazine by the legendary comedian Ernie Kovacs, who was a die-hard *MAD* fan.

"Gopo Gossum!" (*MAD* #23, May 1955, illustrated by Wallace Wood) is Kurtzman's look at *Pogo*, Walt Kelly's venerable syndicated strip, which was created in 1948. Set in the Okeefenokee Swamp, it featured such unique characters as Pogo Possum, Albert the Alligator, Churchy LaFemme (a turtle), and Howland Owl. Immensely popular, the politically satirical *Pogo* was expanded into both comic books and a best-selling series of paperbacks. *Pogo*, incidentally, rivaled *MAD* in popularity on college campuses of the period. In the fifties, numerous undergrads (and a fair amount of their professors) could be observed wearing "I Go Pogo" buttons to class. For his part, Wood seems to have realized that he absolutely nailed Walt Kelly's drawing style here—note that the tag line at the bottom of the first panel reads "Copied right 1954 by Walt Wood." Senator Joe McCarthy, who was first seen in *MAD* in "What's My Shine?" (see *The MAD Reader)*, returns for a cameo appearance here.

The 1933 RKO Pictures classic *King Kong* is lampooned by Kurtzman in "Ping Pong!" (*MAD* #6, August-September 1953, illustrated by Bill Elder). While the then-twenty-year-old *King Kong* was not new, it certainly was ingrained enough in the public's imagination for Kurtzman to parody. (The film may also have been in re-release at the time.) In this story Elder takes his "side gags" to new heights; there are enough of them here to merit a separate reading through the story in order to catch them all. And Kurtzman's surprise ending is, as we have come to expect, inspired *MAD*ness.

Art credit unavailable (late 1960s)

"Poopeye!" (*MAD* #21, March 1955, illustrated by Bill Elder) is, of course, Kurtzman's poke at everyone's favorite spinach-eating sailor, Popeye. Created and illustrated by E.C. Segar in 1929, Popeye actually began life as a walk-on character in a King Features comic strip called *Thimble Theatre*. He didn't make his first appearance until ten years into the strip's run, but once Popeye came he never left—he was an immediate hit with readers. In 1931 the strip's name was amended to *Thimble Theatre Starring Popeye*.

The strip proved to be a merchandising bonanza, spawning numerous spin-offs, including cartoons, toys, comic books, and (much later) even a feature film written by Jules Feiffer, directed by Robert Altman, and starring Robin Williams as Popeye.

"Smithson John and Co." originally appeared as the bottom section of the typeset cover to *MAD* #21 (March 1955), and is Kurtzman's parody of the Johnson Smith and Co. ads that regularly appeared in comic books and magazines of the time. Kurtzman was particularly proud of his work on this piece, telling comics historian John Benson that "about a year's worth of writing went into that cover. Every sentence is funny." Johnson Smith and Co. is still in business, selling "Things You Never Knew Existed!"

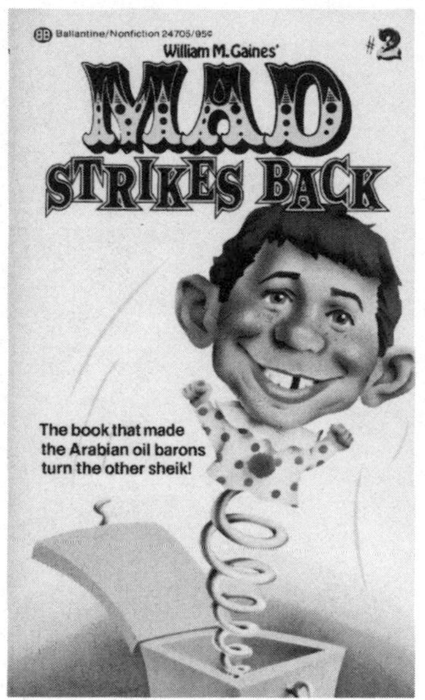

Art by Robert Grossman (1975)

"Teddy and the Pirates!" (*MAD* #6, August-September 1953, illustrated by Wallace Wood) spoofs the popular adventure strip *Terry and the Pirates*. Begun in 1934 by artist/writer Milton Caniff, Terry was, according to the first installment of the strip, a "wide awake American boy whose grandfather left him a map of an abandoned mine in China." Terry's companions on his adventures included Pat Ryan, a "two-fisted adventurer," the Chinese guide Connie, a gang of Chinese pirates headed by Poppy Joe, and a femme fatale known as the Dragon Lady. Caniff left the strip in 1946 to create *Steve Canyon*, and passed the feature along to George Wunder, who worked on it until it was finally canceled in 1973. In "Teddy and the Pirates," Kurtzman sets up a recurring question ("I wonder why you're called 'Teddy and the Pirates?' ") that propels the story to its climax, a technique he often employed in the *MAD* comic.

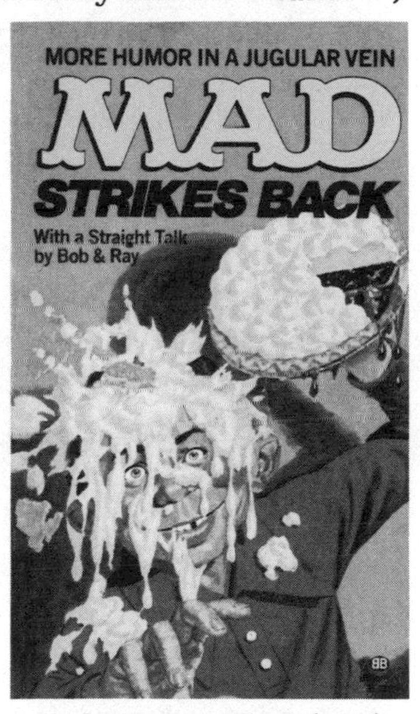

Art by Norman Mingo (1976)

Jack Davis, who loved drawing westerns, was the perfect artist to illustrate "Cowboy!" (*MAD* #20, February 1955), which is Kurtzman's western lampoon. The device employed here, side-by-side comparisons of the fictionalized version and the real-life one, is a technique Kurtzman used numerous times over the course of his work in *MAD*. Davis's art is so effective that you can almost *smell* the "real-life" cowboys.

The closing slot in *MAD Strikes Back!* is occupied by "Manduck the Magician" (*MAD* #14, August 1954, illustrated by Bill Elder). The object of this parody, *Mandrake the Magician*, was created in 1934 by writer Lee Falk and artist Phil Davis; the strip was distributed by King Features Syndicate. Mandrake was a magician/crime fighter who used his wits and powers of prestidigitation to right wrongs. He also employed the powers of hypnosis to trick dim-witted criminals. Mandrake's sidekick was Lothar, who sported a fez and a leopard-skin tunic; Lothar was the first black character with a major recurring role to appear in an adventure strip. Kurtzman was always looking for ways to push the envelope; note that about halfway through the story, he employs the use of "found images." For this he had to look no farther than his own backyard: the photos of bodybuilder Charles Atlas ("Let me give you a new he-man body!") used in the story were taken from actual paid ads that were then appearing on the back cover of all the E.C. comics, including *MAD*.

"The Men Who Make *MAD*" page, first seen at the end of *The MAD Reader*, appears here as well. As with the similar page in *The MAD Reader*, this was eventually dropped from the numerous later printings of *MAD Strikes Back!*

Fifty years later, the material that comprises this volume is being reprinted, not just for historical purposes, but for the same reason it was originally successful: it's funny. *MAD*-ly funny!

Grant Geissman *is the author of* Collectibly MAD, *(Kitchen Sink Press, 1995), and co-author with Fred von Bernewitz of* Tales of Terror! The EC Companion *(Gemstone/Fantagraphics, 2000). He compiled and annotated the "best of" volumes* MAD About the Fifties *(Little, Brown, 1997),* MAD About the Sixties *(Little, Brown, 1995),* MAD About the Seventies *(Little, Brown, 1996), and* MAD About the Eighties *(Rutledge Hill Press, 1999). He compiled and wrote liner notes for* MAD Grooves *(Rhino, 1996), and also contributed the introduction to* Spy vs. Spy: The Complete Casebook *(Watson-Guptill, 2001). When not reading* MAD, *Geissman is a busy Hollywood studio guitarist, composer, and "contemporary jazz" recording artist with 11 highly regarded albums released under his own name.*

Straight Talk from BOB & RAY

BOB ELLIOTT RAY GOULDING

First of all, we would like to congratulate the beloved folks who make "Mad" possible, for having the courage to bring out this second volume. The reader will certainly be further encouraged by the fact that these same people showed the extreme good taste to invite us to forward this work.

(The only actual experience we've had in forwarding a book was when we returned a borrowed copy of The United States Armed Forces Institute textbook, "Air-Conditioning II" to its rightful owner.)

At the outset, we should mention that we've devoted a great deal of our time to *not* reading forwards to books; probably, together, we have spent more time not reading forwards than any other two people in radio *or* television.

An important thing to check, incidentally, before reading any book, is the Library of Congress Catalog Card Number. Often, when people learn that we do this, they say, "Why bother with that, Bob and Ray?"

To which we answer, "Because it's efficient. It avoids confusion."

Supposing the Library of Congress Catalog Card number is "55-5968." The first two digits represent the year of publication, as any fool can figure out. But taking the next four numbers in pairs, you find that 5 and 9 make 14, while 6 and 8 also total 14. 14 and 14 are 28, which you divide by 4 (which is how many digits there are, following the year of publication), and you get 7. 7, then, is your key number.

Now, when you get to the Library of Congress, you say to the nice librarian, "Get me Number Seven, please." The nice librarian quickly does some mental calculating. She knows seven goes into twenty-eight 4 times, which is her clue to the number of digits

Scene of Bob and Ray doing their fantastic imitations which are unbelievably difficult to differentiate from the genuine voices.

following the year of publication. Dividing the digits into pairs she gets "2," and "2" goes into twenty-eight 14 times. Two combinations of 14, (five and nine; six and eight) give her 55-5968, and she goes and gets "Trumpeter's Tale."—(The Story of Young Louis Armstrong) by Jeanette Eaton. No waste of time, no delay. Efficiency.

We could go on with stories like this about all of our friends at "Mad" but then the forward would become the book. Naturally you don't want that, and neither do we. Besides, Simon and Schuster has been trying to get a book out of us for three years, and if we write any book, it'll be for them.

So now, let's all turn with gay anticipation to the opening pages of this volume, with the words of Edgar A. Guest still ringing in our ears:

"It takes a heap of homeing
To make a pigeon toed."

Glad we could get together! Good night . . . and good luck!

BOB ELLIOTT signs off with his, "Write if you get work."

RAY GOULDING's cheery tip is: "Hang by your thumbs."

MAD
strikes back!

Greetings, dear Reader! . . . All settled for a comfortable evening of reading? . . .That's it! . . . Settle down! . . . Snuggle into your favorite curbstone! . . . all comfy now? . . . Well enjoy it while you can, Kid, 'cause after reading this book, you'll be a nervous wreck! And our book starts with . . .

YOUNG PRINCE VIOLENT OF DRULE WHO ASPIRETH TO BECOMETH A KNIGHTETH AT-ETH KINGETH ARTHURETH ROUTH... RATH... THOOTH... PTOOEY!...AT KING ARTHUR'S ROUND TABLE, WHILES AWAY THE TIME IN GREAT FUN AT THE SPORT OF MOCK COMBAT!... WITH DULL-EDGED WOODEN SWORDS AND PADDED DOUBLETS, PRINCE VIOLENT, IN GREAT FUN AND SPORT... SCORES A BLOW IN FUN UPON HIS GOOD FRIEND AND HAS SO MUCH FUN!... BOY WHAT FUN!... FUN! WOW!... FUN!
WOOD

CRUNCH!
...BUT IF ONE LOOKS CLOSELY AT THE PRINCE WHO IS TROMP-ING SPORTINGLY ON HIS FALLEN FRIEND, ONE SEES THAT HE IS NOT HAPPY!

...ONE SEES BY THE WAYS HE LANDS ON HIS TOES INSTEAD OF HIS HEELS... THE HEELS WITH THE 'TAPS'!...THAT HIS HEART IS NOT WITH THIS GREAT SPORT!

...FOR THE YOUNG MAN'S HEART IS FILLED WITH OTHER LONGINGS!... YES...THE LONGINGS THAT USUALLY FILL A YOUNG MAN'S HEART WHEN WINTER TURNS TO SPRING...
1

Boing!
...YES...IN SPRING HIS YOUNG MAN'S FANCY TURNS, OF COURSE, TO HIS BUTTERFLY COLLECTION WHICH HE HOPETH TO COMPLETE THIS SPRING! THEN... AS THE PRINCE LEAPETH (TO STOMPETH) TOO HIGH...HE IS SMITTEN BY A VISION AND A CEILING!
whuf!
...A VISION OF A BEAUTIFUL GIRL NAMED ALOTA! AND OF LONG GOLDEN HAIR SHE HAS ALOTA!... THIS IS THE WOMAN OF PRINCE VIOLENT'S DREAMS AND IN A MOMENT, HE TRYETH TO PURSUETH, BUT HE GETS STUCKETH!

ALAS...HIS LANCE DOES NOT FIT SIDEWAYS THROUGH THE PORTCULIS! AND WHEN HE FINALLY FIGURES IT OUT AND TRAMPS ACROSS THE DRAW-BRIDGE, THE MAIDEN IS GONETH!

...AND PRINCE VIOLENT HAS BARELY LEFT THE CASTLE OF HIS FATHER WHEN HIS TROUBLES BEGIN!... HE IS CAUGHT WITH HIS STEED IN THE GRIP OF SOME FORCE...

...THAT PULLS HORSE AND RIDER BACKWARDS! 'INDEED, THIS IS WITCHCRAFT', VIOL THINKS TO HIMSELF! (WE'LL CALL HIM 'VIOL' OR 'VILE' FOR SHORT!)

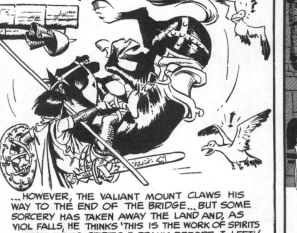

...HOWEVER, THE VALIANT MOUNT CLAWS HIS WAY TO THE END OF THE BRIDGE... BUT SOME SORCERY HAS TAKEN AWAY THE LAND AND, AS VIOL FALLS, HE THINKS 'THIS IS THE WORK OF SPIRITS ...INTOXICATING SPIRITS I DRANK BEFORE I LEFT'!
...BUT A MOMENT LATER... QUIETLY PONDERING AMIDST THE STENCH OF THE MOAT... VIOL SEES IT IS NEITHER SPIRITS NOR WITCHCRAFT BUT MERELY THE SLANTED DRAWBRIDGE WHICH HATH RISETH BY ACCIDENTETH WHILE HE WAS ON-ETH!
2

AND SO, AFTER HE GOETH BACK HOME AND CHANGETH HIS RUSTY CHAIN MAIL FOR A FRESH-PRESSED, CRISP, OILED CHAIN-MAIL, HE DOTH SET OUT UPON THE HIGH-ROAD!
...SEEKING DIRECTIONS AS TO WHICH WAY ALOTA HATH GONE, PRINCE VIOLENT STOPPETH A MAN WHOM, BY HIS POINTY-SHAPED HELMET, VIOL TAKETH TO BE A SOLDIER!
one way
rap! rap!

IMAGINE VIOL'S SURPRISE WHEN HE DISCOVERETH THE VARLET HATH NO HELMET ON AT ALL! THE MAN POINTETH OUT WHERE THE MAIDEN HATH PASSED...

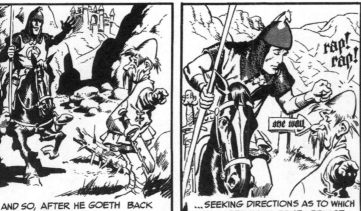

...PRINCE VIOLENT SETS OUT IN THE DIRECTION THAT HAS BEEN POINTETH BY THE MAN WHOSE HEAD HAS ALSO BEEN POINTETH!... AFTER MANY WEARY DAYS OF JOURNEYING, VIOL'S HEART LEAPS AS HE CATCHES A GLIMPSE OF LONG GOLDEN HAIR!... *ALOTA!*

KISS
KISS
KISS
KISS
...AND IT IS ONLY WHEN HE HAS SKIPPED OVER AND SWEPT THE HAIR TO HIS LIPS... IT IS ONLY *THEN* THAT THE BURRS, THE UNWASHED SMELL, THE LITTLE *MOVING* THINGS TELL HIM THAT THIS IS NOT A *MAIDEN'S* HAIR BUT A WARRIOR'S *BEARD!*

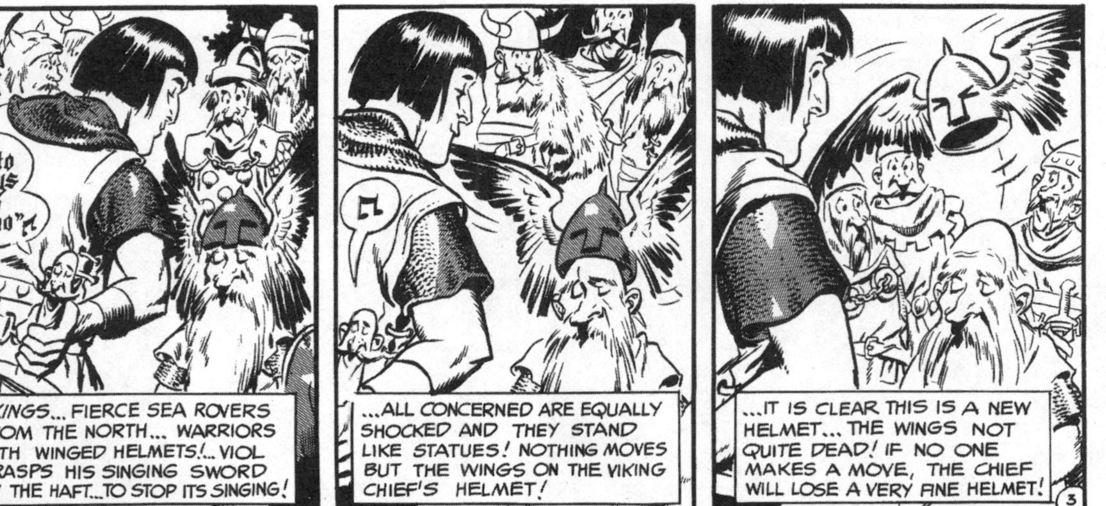
"veto says "no no"
VIKINGS... FIERCE SEA ROVERS FROM THE NORTH... WARRIORS WITH WINGED HELMETS!... VIOL GRASPS HIS SINGING SWORD BY THE HAFT... TO STOP ITS SINGING!
...ALL CONCERNED ARE EQUALLY SHOCKED AND THEY STAND LIKE STATUES! NOTHING MOVES BUT THE WINGS ON THE VIKING CHIEF'S HELMET!
...IT IS CLEAR THIS IS A NEW HELMET... THE WINGS NOT QUITE DEAD! IF NO ONE MAKES A MOVE, THE CHIEF WILL LOSE A VERY FINE HELMET!
3

VIOL REACTS SWIFTLY AND IN ONE SMOOTH MOTION, DRAWS ARROW FROM QUIVER...DROPS ARROW... PICKS UP ARROW... DROPS BOW... DROPS ARROW...PICKS UP BOW... DROPS QUIVER...PICKS UP STUFF AND SMOOTHLY SKEWERS THE HELMET...
...AFTER TWELVE SHOTS, THAT IS!... VIOL'S NEAT SHOT DROPS THE HELMET! HE PICKS UP THE HELMET AND DROPS THE QUIVER... PICKS UP QUIVER... DROPS HELMET AND BOW... PICKS UP BOW...DROPS QUIVER, HELMET, BOW, ARROW, CHAIN MAIL, PANTS...
thud!

ka-pweeng!
...THE VIKING CHIEF, OVER JOYEDETH AT THE RETURN-ETH OF HIS HELMET... POINTETH OUT TO VIOL A MAIDEN WITH GOLDEN HAIR WHO SITTETH BY THE DOCK IN A VIKING ROW-BOAT! VIOL JOYOUSLY POUNDS DOWN TO THE SHORE TO JOINETH!

splash!
... AND AS VIOL HASTENS TO JOINETH THE ROW-BOAT, THE ROW-BOAT HASTENS TO JOINETH THE OPPOSITE SHORE... AND AGAIN, PRINCE VIOLENT HATH TAKEN A FLYING-FLOP INTO THE WATER! FOR SOME REASON, THE MAID, ALOTA, IS AVOIDING HIM!

...THE VIKINGS HATH AGREED TO CARRY VIOL ACROSS THE LAKE, BUT FIRST HE GOETH BACK HOME TO CHANGETH HIS RUSTY CHAIN MAIL FOR CRISP, OILED CHAIN MAIL!

EEEYOW!
VERILY, THE DRY-CLEANERS DOTH DO A GOOD BUSINESS! ANY-HOW, THE VIKINGS DOTH TAKE VIOL ACROSS THE LAKE WHERE HE IS SMITTEN BY A TERRIBLE PAIN!

munch
shmeg
FOR YOU SEE, VIOL HATH COME TOO CLOSE TO THE TERRIBLE FIGUREHEAD IN THE PROW OF THE VIKING SHIP AS HE DONE STEPPETH ASHORE!
4

help!
PURSUING HIS QUEST, VIOL STANDETH ON A SUM-
MIT IN A HEROIC POSTURE!... NOT THAT THIS SUMMIT
OVERLOOKS ANYTHING, SINCE IT FACETH A ROCK WALL
...BUT HOBOY... WHAT A HEROIC POSTURE! SUDDENLY
VIOL'S SINGING SWORD STARTS SHRIEKING!

help help!
Achtung!
... VIOL LOOKS OVER HIS SHOULDER TO SEE-ETH WHAT
MAKES THE SWORD SHRIEKETH INSTEAD OF SINGETH!
... DOWN BELOW, FILING THROUGH A DEFILE IN THE
VALLEY IS A PARTY OF THOSE FIERCE WARRIORS
THAT SWARM OVER EUROPE... HUNS!

THE HUNS ATTACK, BUT VIOL MEETETH THEM WITH HIS RAZOR-SHARP SINGING SWORD, HOLLOW-GROUND!... (EDITOR'S NOTE: IN THE INTERESTETH OF CLEANER COMICS, WE HAVE AVOIDED SHOWING BLOOD AND GUTS, BUT WE SUGGEST THAT YOU DROOLING READERS MERELY FOLLOW THE SLASHES WHERE SHIELDS, HELMETS, ETC., ARE CUT!... THEN USE YOUR IMAGINATION TO FIGURE OUT HOW GRISLEY THE UNSEEN FLESH-CUTS ARE, AND YOU WILL GET AS GOOD AN EFFECT AS IF YOU SAW REGULAR BLOOD AND GUTS!)

WHEN HUNS SEE HUNS HE
HACK, MANY TAKE REFUGE
BEHIND A HUGE STURDY OAK!
BUT VIOL, HE HACK THEM HUNS
SAME AS HOW HE HACK HALF!

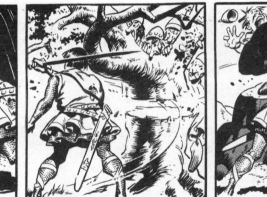

there is nothing like a dame...
troll bridge
NOW VIOL SHEATHES HIS FABULOUS SWORD IN ITS ORNATE, ENCRUSTED SCABBARD... ITS ORNATE, CRUD ENCRUSTED SCABBARD, AND WHILE STRIKING A HEROIC POSTURE ON A CONVENIENT WINDBLOWN SUMMIT, HE SEES *KING ARTHUR'S CASTLE* AND THE FAIR MAID *ALOTA* HURRYING TOWARDS IT!
SHE GOETH INSIDE AND VIOL, ATTEMPTING TO FOLLOW, IS BARRED BY A WELL-MEANING KNIGHT, WHO CHALLENGES VIOL BY THE TIME-HONORED CUSTOM OF TAKING OFF HIS HEAVY, STEEL GAUNTLETED, RIVETED, IRON BOUND GLOVE AND THROWING IT TO THE GROUND!

UNFORTUNATELY, IT LANDETH ON PRINCE VIOLENT'S TOE AND IT IS SOME TIME BEFORE HE GAINS HIS COMPOSURE ENOUGH TO PREPARE FOR COMBAT! FORTUNATELY FOR HIM, THE CUSTOM IS NOT YET IN VOGUE FOR A CHALLENGER TO SLAP THE *FACE* WITH THE GLOVE!

Schmehen heimer
cut-rate armor
ALBEIT... THE CONTESTANTS PREPARE TO TILT... TILT, BEING THE WORD THAT DESCRIBETH THE JOUST OR MOUNTED CONTEST...NOT TO BE CONFUSETH WITH THE PIN-BALL MACHINE CONTEST!... THE PONDEROUS ARMOR IS BROUGHT ON A GROANING WHEEL-BARROW!

...FIRST A HAUBURK, A HEAVY COAT OF HAM-MERED-LINK CHAIN-MAIL IS FITTED OVER THE CONTESTANTS' TUNICS...

...THEN THE THICK, PROTECTIVE IRON CUIRASS AND THE WEIGHTY IRON LEG PROTECTORS ARE TIED...

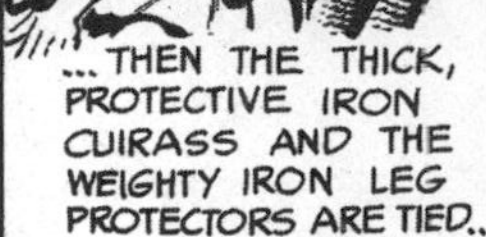
...NEXT THE HEAVY... THICKEST-OF-ALL PIECE OF IRON... THE HEUME OR HELMET, DROPPED OVER THE GORGET WITH A KLANK!

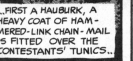

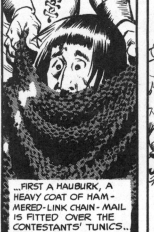

THE ARMORED WARRIORS, TOO WEIGHTED DOWN TO MOVE ARE PAIN-FULLY HOISTED OVER THEIR MOUNTS...

...AND EASED ONTO THE HEAVILY ARMORED HORSES WHERE THEY RECEIVE THE MIGHTY LANCE, THE HUGE TWO-HANDED SWORD, THE BATTLE AXE, THE MACE AND A COUPLE DOZEN DAGGERS! AND NOW?... NOW?...
YOU KNOW WHAT HAPPENS NOW?...

ker-rumf!
nay!
neigh!
...THE WHOLE FURSHLUGGINER MESS COL-LAPSES LIKE A PACK OF CARDS!

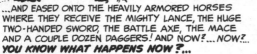

THOUGH VIOL IS PINNED FAST BY HIS PRODIGIOUS ARMOR, HE IS MADE OF STURDIER STUFF...
...QUICKER THAN IT TAKES TO TELL, HIS RIGHT INDEX FINGER, WHICH IS FREE, WRIGGLES FORWARD...
...AND WITH A WILD CRY, THE INDEX FINGER LEAPS UPON THE ENEMY'S INDEX FINGER!
...BOTH HANDS ROLL OVER AND OVER THRASHING UP A CLOUD OF DUST WHICH HIDES THE FEARFUL COMBAT!

ALL THROUGH THE AFTERNOON THEY BATTLE, BUT FINALLY, DUE TO VIOL'S CLEAN LIVING, 100% AMERICANISM, AND HE DOESN'T BITE HIS NAILS... HE DOTH GET A GRIP THAT HIS ENEMY CANNOT BREAKETH AND VIOL WINS THE THUMB-WRESTLE!

higher sire?
I'll see thee.
who dealt this mess?
PRINCE VIOLENT IS THEN SUMMONED TO THE FABULOUS ROUND TABLE WHERE KING ARTHUR SITTETH WITH HIS KNIGHTS TO DISCUSS BATTLES, TO DISCUSS GLORIOUS DEEDS, TO DISCUSS VICTORIES, BUT MAINLY TO PLAYETH CARDS!
7

BUT KING ARTHUR DISCOVERETH THAT THE TABLE IS NOT TRULY ROUND BUT SLIGHTLY OVAL, SO HE ABANDONETH!... BESIDES, HE WANTETH TO QUIT GAME WHILE STILL AHEAD!... THEN HE TURNETH TO VIOL WHO IS IN TYPICAL HEROIC POSTURE!

FOR VIOL'S GLORIOUS DEEDS AND VICTORIES, KING ARTHUR DECIDES TO KNIGHTETH AND HE RAISES HIS SWORD AND BRINGS IT DOWN TO DUB VIOL KNIGHT!... UNFORTUNATELY, HE USETH *EDGE* OF SWORD INSTEAD OF *FLAT*...

oops!
...SPLITTING THE KNEELING FIGURE BEFORE HIM IN TWAIN! HOWEVER, THE KNEELING FIGURE IS THE BOOT-BLACK WHO KNEELETH TO POLISH THE KING'S BOOTS!... HAPPILY, VIOL HATH CAUGHT SIGHT OF THE SHY MAIDEN, ALOTA, AND PURSUETH!

FINALLY HE CORNERETH AND ASKETH HER WHY SHE HATH RUNNETH AWAY ALL THE TIME, AND AS IF HIS HAIRY CHEST, BRISTLING THROUGH HIS BATTLE TORN GARMENTS HATH GIVEN HER THE ANSWER, SHE WHIPPETH OUT A SCISSOR...

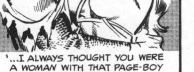

...VIOL, WHO SEES THE WILD LOOK SHE GIVES HIS CHEST, SHRINKS TO DEFEND THE SINGLE HAIR THAT GROWETH THEREON... BUT HE IS NOT QUICK ENOUGH!

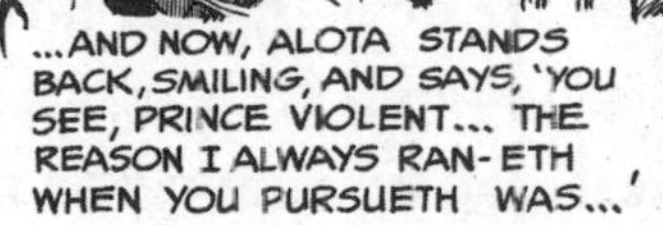

...AND NOW, ALOTA STANDS BACK, SMILING, AND SAYS, 'YOU SEE, PRINCE VIOLENT... THE REASON I ALWAYS RAN-ETH WHEN YOU PURSUETH WAS...'

'...I ALWAYS THOUGHT YOU WERE A WOMAN WITH THAT PAGE-BOY BOB YOU WORE!...NOW I SEE YOU ARE A MAN!'... THEY KISSETH!...OUR STORY ENDETH!
8

Are you sick of television? Do you watch television from morning till night and finally, in desperation, you run out and buy a comic book to get your mind off of television? . . . Well, this story . . . for you readers who are truly sick of seeing television, television, television . . . this story will make you sicker, because it's more about television! . . . this story about . . .

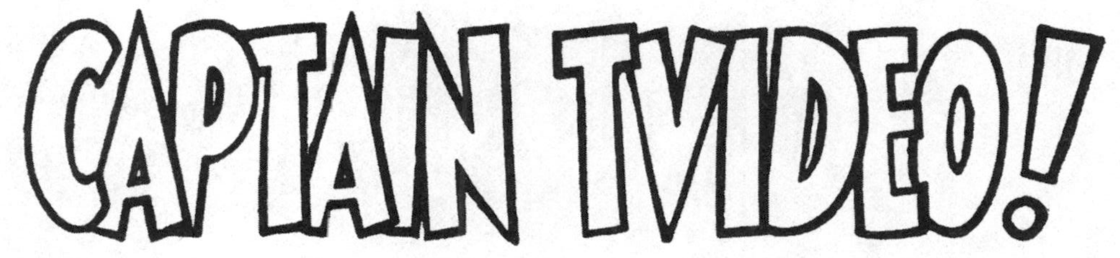

...AND NOW, THE LATEST ADVENTURE, '**THE MISSING ARMS OF VENUS**'... VENUS THE PLANET, THAT IS!
CAPTAIN TVIDEO IS **BLASTING OFF** TO SEE THE SPACE COMMISSIONER! IT IS MORNING!... HOWEVER IT LOOKS LIKE EVENING 'CAUSE YOU DON'T HAVE THE 'BRIGHT' CONTROL TURNED UP ENOUGH!
JACK DAVIS

...A FEW MOMENTS LATER, CAPTAIN TVIDEO BLASTS BACK ON OUTSIDE THE COMMISSIONER'S OFFICE WHERE HE BLASTS-IN THROUGH THE DOOR AND BLASTS-OUT...
...EH? ...EH?
...WHAT'S THAT YOU SAY, CAPTAIN TVIDEO?...EH? ...EH?...EH?
...HA!...I KNOW WHY I CAN'T HEAR YOU!... YOU'VE GOT YOUR 'ROCKET-RANGER' SPACE HELMET ON!

...HAVING TROUBLE GETTING IT OFF, CAPTAIN?
...NNGH! ...NNGH!
...FURSHLUGGINER PROP MEN BUY THESE KID SPACE HELMETS IN THE 5 AND 10...
...WHEN'S THIS SHOW GONNA GET A DECENT BUDGET?

...NOW, LET'S GO ABOUT THIS CALMLY AND RATIONALLY!...SURELY, BY THE THOUGHTFUL USE OF MODERN TOOLS AND EQUIPMENT, WE CAN REMOVE THAT SPACE HELMET!
YOU DON'T HAFTA! YOU DON'T HAFTA!

...SURELY BY THE DELICATE, SKILLFUL USE OF MAN'S CLEVERLY DESIGNED MACHINES, WE CAN DEFTLY REMOVE THAT SPACE HELMET... LIKE FER-INSTANCE... ***IF I BASH IT WITH ALL MY MIGHT WITH A MONKEY WRENCH!***
YOU DON'T HAFTA... YOU DON'T HAFTA!
CRASH

...I SAY, CAPTAIN TVIDEO!...YOU **DID** MANAGE TO PULL THE HELMET OFF **AFTER** ALL!...SORRY IF I ACTED TOO HASTILY!
POK
POK
POK
...I **TOLD** YOU YOU DIDN'T HAFTA!
WELL, NEVER MIND, COMMISSIONER... LET'S **BLAST-DOWN** TO BUSINESS! I HEAR TELL THAT ARMS ARE BEING SHIPPED HERE FROM VENUS... THE PLANET, THAT IS! I NEED YOUR HELP, COMMISSIONER!
...BUT FIRST, I'D BETTER ALERT MY RANGERS WITH THE 'RANGER ALERTER' SWITCH...
THE ROCKET MODEL...
HAS ESCAPED!
WAIT... WAIT...
KETCH IT!

FRROOSH!
...THAT'S NOT THE 'RANGER ALERTER' SWITCH!... THAT'S THE STUDIO FIRE-HOSE SWITCH!... THIS PAPER STAPLER IS THE 'RANGER ALERTER' SWITCH!
O.K.! ...HERE GOES MY RANGER ALERT!
...MEANWHILE, I'LL BRIEF YOU ON WHAT'S HAPPENED!... ALIEN CREATURES ON VENUS, WHO CAN BE INVISIBLE TO THE EARTHIAN EYE, HAVE THE PROPERTY OF SINKING INTO AN EARTHIAN HUMAN BODY SO THAT THE EARTHIAN BODY WILL THINK WITH AN ALIEN VENUSIAN MIND!
CLEP
CLEP
CLEP
CLEP

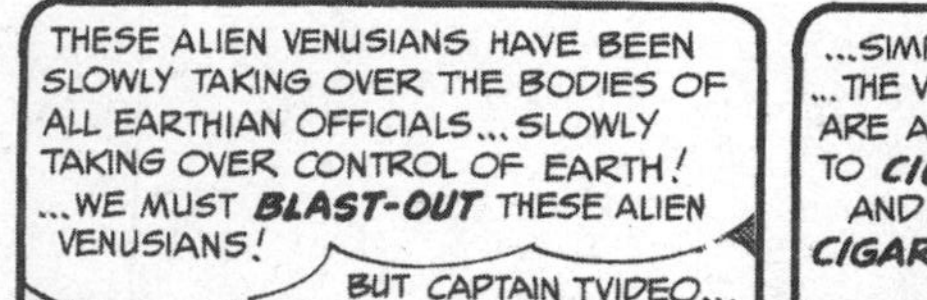
THESE ALIEN VENUSIANS HAVE BEEN SLOWLY TAKING OVER THE BODIES OF ALL EARTHIAN OFFICIALS... SLOWLY TAKING OVER CONTROL OF EARTH! ...WE MUST **BLAST-OUT** THESE ALIEN VENUSIANS!
BUT CAPTAIN TVIDEO... HOW CAN WE RECOGNIZE THOSE WHOSE BODIES ARE INVADED BY THE ALIEN VENUSIANS?
SNIFF!
...SIMPLE! ...THE VENUSIANS ARE ADDICTED TO **CIGARS** AND **CIGARETTES!**
...MY DEAR TVID'... IGNORING THE FACT THAT THIS STORY PLOT IS MISERABLE HACK... I CANNOT BE IMPRESSED BY THIS ADDICTION ANGLE! ...WHY... **MOST EARTHIANS** (**EVEN I**) ARE ADDICTED TO CIGARS AND CIGARETTES!
SLERP!

AHA! ...BUT IT'S THE **PECULIAR WAY** THAT THEY ARE ADDICTED TO CIGARS AND CIGARETTES THAT GIVES THEM AWAY!
...MY GOOD FELLOW... YOUR STORY SOUNDS QUITE RIDICULOUS TO ME! WHY... WHAT COULD **POSSIBLY** BE PECULIAR ABOUT CIGAR AND CIGARETTE ADDICTION? (UMP... CHOMP... GULP)... I SAY... THESE CORONA-CORONAS **ARE** DE-LICIOUS... (CHOMP... ULP)!
CHOMP!

EATING CIGARS AND CIGARETTES IS PECULIAR, 'COMMISSIONER', ALIAS 'DIRTY UNAMERICAN ALIEN VENUSIAN'?... KEEP YOUR HAND OUT OF YOUR POCKET BECAUSE THIS SPARKLER I HAVE IN MY HAND IS A NUCLEAR BLAST-OFF GUN!... NO YOU DON'T...
OH YEAH! ...WELL THIS FLASHLIGHT IS ACTUALLY A HYDROGEN-OXIDE-OXYGEN RAY... OR A H.O.O.-RAY...
NYEH
ZAP
ZAP
..GOT 'IM!
...I'D BETTER CALL MY ASSISTANT RANGER AND BLAST-OFF TO BLAST VENUS, RIGHT AWAY!
...NOW THIS FLASHLIGHT MUST BE A MICROPHONE!
... CAPTAIN TVIDEO CALLING ASSISTANT RANGER...
TIYO KIMOSAVEE! ...YOU WANT ME?
...ASSISTANT RANGER... NOT LONE RANGER!

AH... MY ASSISTANT RANGER WITH YOUR SPACE HELMET ON! ... I KNOW... IT'S STUCK AND YOU CAN'T GET IT OFF!... WELL... DON'T WORRY!... I LEARNED A SIMPLE WAY TO GET IT OFF... BANG IT WITH ALL MY MIGHT WITH A MONKEY WRENCH!
... YOU DON'T HAFTA!... YOU DON'T HAFTA!
STOP ETT!
SNAG IT!
KETCH THET THING!
...I SAY, ROCKET-RANGER, YOU DON'T HAVE A SPACE HELMENT ON AFTER ALL ... MERELY A PIECE OF CUT OUT LAUNDRY-SHIRT CARDBOARD WITH A HELMET PAINTED ON IT! ...DID I HURT YOU?
...ONLY WHEN I LAUGH!
...OKAY!... ALL KIDDING ASIDE!... WE'VE GOT TO CARRY THIS WAR TO VENUS!... LOAD YOUR SPARKLER WITH FLINTS AND COME OUT TO THE ROCKET-SHIP WHERE WE SHALL PREPARE TO BLAST-OFF!

...AND SO... WITH THE IMMORTAL WORDS OF '**BLAST-OFF**' ECHOING HOLLOWLY IN THE COMMISSIONER'S OFFICE, THE SCENE FADES OUT...

...AND THE NEXT SCENE THAT FADES IN IS A BRAND NEW SCENE THAT TAKES PLACE IN CAPTAIN TVIDEO'S ROCKET SHIP!

...ACTUALLY, IT'S THE SAME OLD SCENE ONLY WITH A FRAME STUCK OVER TO LOOK LIKE IT'S A NEW SCENE IN A ROCKET SHIP!
...CAPTAIN! I'M SCARED! ARE YOU?

...SCARED?... LISTEN, RANGER!... THERE HASN'T BEEN A SINGLE SOLDIER... A SINGLE HUMAN BEING... WHO... GOING INTO BATTLE... HAS NOT BEEN SCARED! AND SO... IN ANSWER TO WHETHER I, CAPT. TVIDEO AM SCARED... THE ANSWER IS...NO!...I'M NOT SCARED!
...BUT CAPTAIN TVIDEO, WE ARE GOING TO FIGHT THE VENUSIANS WHO HAVE A SUPERIOR CIVILIZATION...HAVE TEN TIMES AS HIGHLY DEVELOPED ARMAMENT... AND VASTLY OUTNUMBER US!... HOW DO YOU PROPOSE TO BEAT THEM?

...ACTUALLY THE CASE WOULD BE QUITE HOPELESS!... HOWEVER I HAVE SOMETHING WITH WHICH I THINK I CAN OUTWIT THEIR SUPERIOR CIVILIZATION...OVER-POWER THEIR HIGHLY DEVELOPED ARMAMENT, AND REDUCE THEIR ABILITY TO OUTNUMBER US!...AND THAT THAT THING IS...THAT THING IS... IS...
...THIS 'ROCKET RANGER'S EMERGENCY RESCUE RING'!
...A 'ROCKET RANGER'S EMERGENCY RESCUE RING'...

...YES... IN A STUNNING PLASTIC FINISH DESIGNED TO FIT ANY FINGER!
...GOSH! WHAT A STUNNING LOOKING RING THAT IS... ONE THAT MY BOY FRIENDS WILL WANT... THAT MY GIRL FRIENDS WILL ADMIRE!
HOW CAN I GET ONE OF THEM RINGS, CAPTAIN TVIDEO?
HOW?
HOW HOW?
...YOU'LL FIND OUT LATER IN THE PROGRAM, RANGER! ... AND NOW, I PUT MY HAND TO THE BLAST-OFF IGNITOR SWITCH... NOW I GET READY TO TURN THE HANDLE ... AND NOW ...
WE BLAST-OFF!
FROOSHT!
OOP! ...TURNED THE STUDIO FIRE-HOSE SWITCH AGAIN!
PLEASE PLEASE!
HOW CAN I GET ONE?
PLEASE!
PLEASE PLEASE PLEASE!

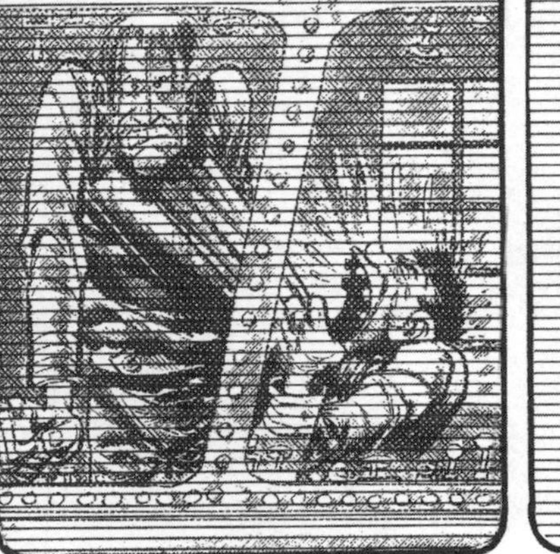

...AND SO... WITH THE ROAR OF THE STUDIO FIRE-HOSE ECHOING HOLLOWLY IN THE ROCKET SHIP, WE LEAVE CAPTAIN TVIDEO...

...LEAVE HIM FOR A MOMENT AS HE ROCKETS TOWARDS VENUS ARMED ONLY WITH THE *'ROCKET RANGER'S EMERGENCY RESCUE RING'*...

GANG!... REMEMBER THE SECRET 'ROCKET RANGER'S EMERGENCY RESCUE RING' THAT CAPTAIN TVIDEO IS IS GOING TO CONQUER VENUS WITH?... WELL NOW WE'VE GOT A **VERY SPECIAL ANNOUNCEMENT** THAT MIGHT PROVE TO BE THE TURNING POINT IN YOUR LIFE!... **AND THAT ANNOUNCEMENT IS...**
STOP ETT
KETCH IT
...YOU... TOO ...CAN... CON-QUER... VENUS!
...YOU...CAN ...GET...ONE...OF ...CAPTAIN ...TVIDEO'S ...'ROCKET RANGER'S EMERGENCY RESCUE RINGS'!

... NOW THIS RING ISN'T ANY **ORDINARY** RING, GANG! FIRST OF ALL, LIKE WE SAID, IT'S STUNNING! IT'S GOT A HEAVY STONE ON TOP SO THAT WHEN YOU'RE IN A FIST FIGHT AND YOU HIT YOUR ENEMY ON THE HEAD WITH THE RING, IT ONLY **STUNS** HIM!... NOW, THAT'S NOT **ALL!** BESIDES HAVING A WHISTLE THAT CAPTAIN TVIDEO ALWAYS USES TO SIGNAL FOR HELP, A COMPASS, A MATCH TO LIGHT A FIRE, AND A MAP OF THE U.S., THIS RING HAS A SECRET POINT THAT SPRINGS OUT... AND **TIPPED WITH POISON**, GANG! ALSO A LITTLE PEEK-HOLE WHERE YOU CAN SEE A CHEESECAKE PICTURE INSIDE!

NOW, GANG, WE'RE MAKING THIS OFFER FOR A VERY LIMITED TIME SO YOU BETTER ACT **NOW** BECAUSE IF YOU DON'T ACT **NOW,** YOU'LL MISS OUT ON THIS HERE OFFER WHICH CLOSES SOON... VERY SOON... AFTER A LIMITED TIME... SOON... SOMETIME IN EARLY 1958!
...NOW WE'RE GIVING THIS RING AWAY ABSOLUTELY FREE WITH THREE DOLLARS TO COVER THE COSTS OF HANDLING AND JUST TWO-HUNDRED WRAPPERS FROM **'GOOKY' CANDY BARS!**
YUM YUM YUMMY YUM
YUM
YUM YUM
HMMM
...YES...**'GOOKY'** CANDY BARS... WITH THAT CRUNCHY-MUNCHY COVERING OF UNSHELLED SUN-FLOWER SEEDS... THAT SMOOTH, MELLOW, TANGY GOLDEN CENTER OF SOFT, CHEWY RUBBER CEMENT... WITH THAT ZESTY, TINGLING, SALTY FLAVOR OF SALT SPRINKLED ON TOP... AND THE RICH, GREEN, SATISFYING COLOR OF 100% U.S. TESTED AND CERTIFIED ARTIFICIAL COLOR!
LAP LAP UMM UMM
GET **'GOOKY'**, AND YOU WILL SAY, LIKE THOUSANDS OF OTHERS, "**OOOH! I GOT 'GOOKY'!**"

...NOW LET US LEAVE THE SIGHT OF A MAN CHEWING HAPPILY ON A 'GOOKY' BAR...THE SOUND OF TEETH MUNCHING INTO THE COVERING...

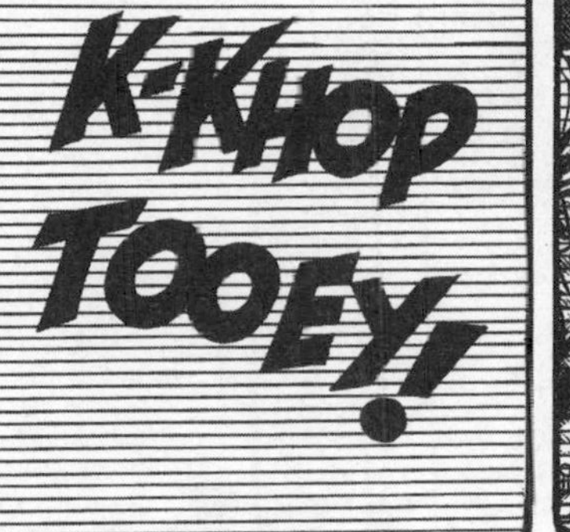
...CRACKLING INTO SUN-FLOWER SEED SHELLS, TWANGING MOMENTARILY ON RUBBER CEMENT!... LET US LEAVE THE SOUND OF REGURGITATING...
K-KHOP TOOEY!

...AND RETURN TO CAPTAIN TVIDEO, WHO...NOW BLASTING-OFF TO VENUS ...FACING THE MOST CRUCIAL HOUR OF HIS WHOLE LIFE... SAYS...
HOW'S YOUR MOM, ED?

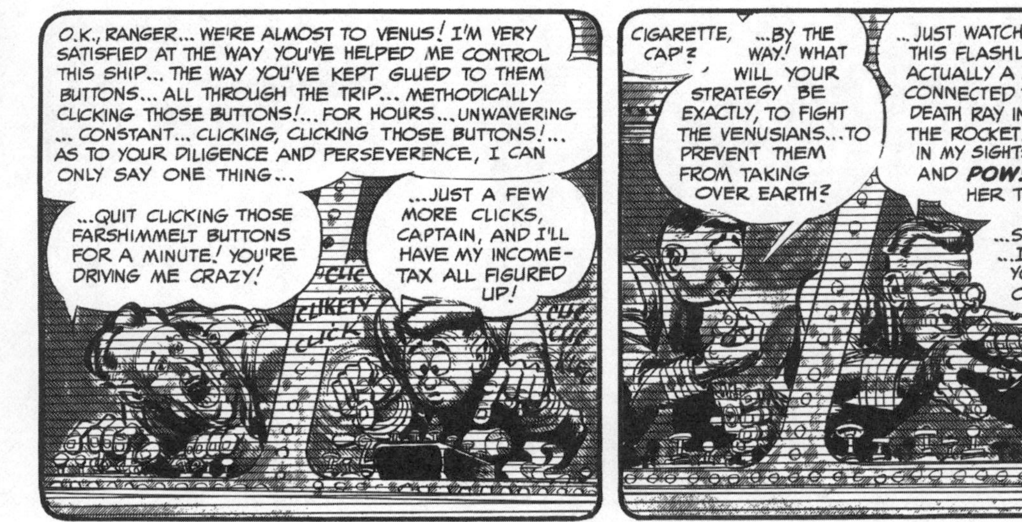
O.K., RANGER... WE'RE ALMOST TO VENUS! I'M VERY SATISFIED AT THE WAY YOU'VE HELPED ME CONTROL THIS SHIP... THE WAY YOU'VE KEPT GLUED TO THEM BUTTONS... ALL THROUGH THE TRIP... METHODICALLY CLICKING THOSE BUTTONS!... FOR HOURS... UNWAVERING ... CONSTANT... CLICKING, CLICKING THOSE BUTTONS!... AS TO YOUR DILIGENCE AND PERSEVERENCE, I CAN ONLY SAY ONE THING...
...QUIT CLICKING THOSE FARSHIMMELT BUTTONS FOR A MINUTE! YOU'RE DRIVING ME CRAZY!
...JUST A FEW MORE CLICKS, CAPTAIN, AND I'LL HAVE MY INCOME-TAX ALL FIGURED UP!
CLIKETY CLICK
CIGARETTE, CAP'?
...BY THE WAY! WHAT WILL YOUR STRATEGY BE EXACTLY, TO FIGHT THE VENUSIANS...TO PREVENT THEM FROM TAKING OVER EARTH?
...JUST WATCH, RANGER! THIS FLASHLIGHT, HERE, IS ACTUALLY A AIMER DEVICE CONNECTED TO A POWERFUL DEATH RAY IN THE NOSE OF THE ROCKET! I GET VENUS IN MY SIGHTS LIKE THIS AND POW!... I BLAST HER TO BITS!
...SAY, RANGER! ...I DIDN'T KNOW YOU SMOKED CIGARETTES!

...I DON'T SMOKE 'EM, CAP'!... I EAT 'EM!
...YES...NOW THAT WE'RE COMING CLOSE TO VENUS... I WAIT TILL SHE'S IN THE CROSS HAIRS AND I PUSH THE BUTTON HERE AND POW!... TAKES COOL NERVES AND CONCENTRATION, SO I DON'T TOUCH CIGARETTES AND I'M SURPRISED THAT YOU DO!... EVERY ROCKET RANGER KNOWS CIGARETTES ARE NO GOOD WHEN YOU SMOKE 'EM OR EAT 'EM...
...EAT 'EM!
...DIRTY UNAMERICAN ALIEN VENUSIAN DISGUISED IN A ROCKET-RANGERS BODY... YOU SHOULD KNOW BETTER THAN TO FOOL WITH CAPTAIN TVIDEO, THE FASTEST DRAW WITH THE NUCLEAR BLAST-OFF GUN! TAKE THIS!

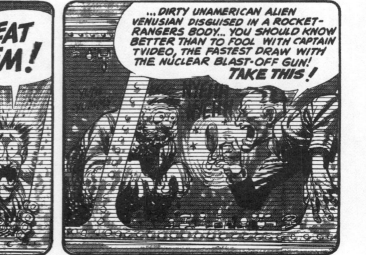

HEY! WO' HOPPEN?
...HEY ROCKET RANGER VENUSIAN!... YOU TURNING INTO GENUINE-LOOKING ALIEN VENUSIAN CREATURE!... **SSST!** WHERE'D YOU GET THAT DISGUISE? **SSST!** THIS AIN'T IN THE SCRIPT! **SSST!** FALL DOWN DEAD! **SSST!** I'M SUPPOSED TO'VE KILLT YOU! **SSST! SSST!**
WO' HOPPEN? WO' HOPPEN?
THESE PROPS!... WHERE'D THEY COME FROM?... LOOKIT... STEEL KNOBS AND DIALS LIKE A REAL ROCKET SHIP! ...WHERE'D WE GET BUDGET FOR SUCH PROPS?
WAIT!... AHA! ...AHAHAH! ...HOOHAA! COULD IT BE? ...THIS STORY PLOT! VENUSIANS TAKING OVER BODIES!... TAKING OVER T.V. ACTORS...

...TAKING OVER WHOLE TELEVISION STUDIOS!... COULD IT REALLY BE? ...FOR HEAVEN'S SAKE, GANG! WARN THE EARTH!... FOR HEAVEN'S SAKE...
FEEP
FEEP

WEC
CHANNEL 5
DOOOOOO

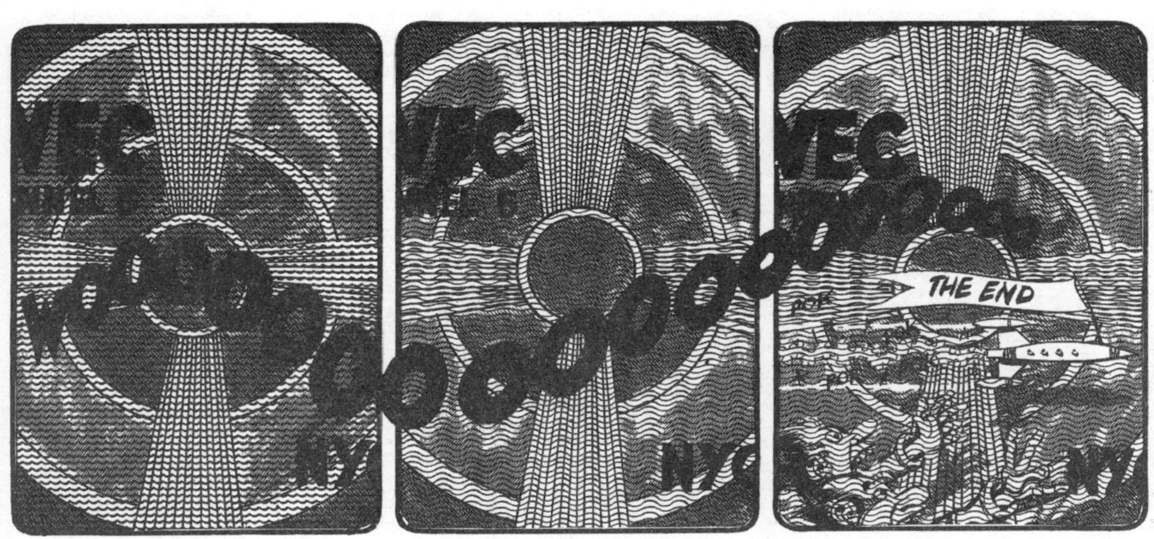
THE END

PUZZLE PAGE!

THE REBUS

HERE IS A POPULAR PUZZLE, GANG, THAT CAN BE ENJOYED BY BOTH KIDDIES AND GROWN-UPS! THE OBJECT IS TO ADD AND SUBTRACT THE LETTERS IN THE NAMES OF THE PICTURED OBJECTS TO GIVE YOU SOME POPULAR WORD VERY OFTEN IN USE IN THE AMERICAN HOUSEHOLD!...

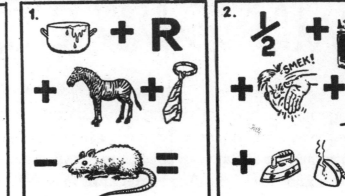

ANSWERS ON LAST PAGE!

The following type of story is the kind where they don't make men act like animals . . . they make the animals act like men! Now why in the heck it's the thing to make animals act like men . . . and it ain't never the fashion to make men act like animals . . . beats us. . . . Anyhow . . .

GOPO GOSSUM!

BY JING! HERE COME LI'L OL GOPO GOSSUM BACK FROM HIS TRIP!
HOWDY, GOPO! COME ALONG AN' JOIN THE FISH-FRY!
RIGHT! WE IS FRYING A MESS OF MIGHTY FINE FISH!
HELP! HELP! CANNIBALS! HOW COME YOU FRYIN' ME? FISHES IS ANIMALS TOO!
THAT'S TRUE! BUT IT GETTIN' HARDER TO CATCH HUMAN-BEINGS ALL THE TIME!
GLMTX
COPIED RIGHT 1954 BY WALT WOOD

HEY, GOPO! WHERE IN THE WORLD YOU BEEN?
I GONE TO CONSORT WITH OUR BIG CITY COUSINS!
"CONSORT"? ... WHAT THAT?
ANY DANG FOOL KNOWS... A "CONSORT" IS WHERE A BUNCH OF MUSICIANS GETS TO-GETHER AND PLAYS HIGH-BROW MUSIC!
NLRB
HEE
NO! NO! THA'S A CONCERT!
A "CONSORT" IS WHERE IN THIS HERE FACTORY THEY GETS ALL DIFFERENT KINDS TIN-CANS AN' SORT OUT THESE CANS WITH THIS HERE MACHINE CALLED A CON SORT!
HOO BOY
THAT A GOOD ONE!
YAK
HAW
YAWK
NBCTY
HYUK
NO! NO! NO! NO! THA'S A CAN-SORT!
... A "CONSORT" IS WHERE THERE'S THIS FELLA NAMED "CON" WHO LOOKED UP IN THE AIR AN' SAW A FLYIN' SAUCER! AN' WHEN ANYBODY ASKED "WHO SAW THE FLYIN' SAUCER?" THEY SAID, "CON SORT!"
HEE
YAK
TWA
HOO
NO! NO! THA'S "CON-SAW IT"!
GEE! WHAT GOOD DRAWING IN THIS STRIP!

PUNS! PUNS! PUNS! THA'S ALL I HEAR ROUN' THIS SWAMP IS PUNS! HOW IN THE EVER-LOVIN' WORLD YOU EXPECT TO HIT THE BIG-TIME JUST SETTIN' ROUND MAKING PUNS!
G*!!π?
I TELL YOU WHY I WENT TO CONSORT (WHICH ACTUALLY MEANS A CERTAIN TYPE OF SWORD) WITH OUR BIG-CITY COUSINS!
I BEEN THINKING... HOW COME OUR COUSINS IS LIVIN' IN 'SPENSIVE PENT-HOUSES WHILE WE LIVIN' IN A FLEA-BITTEN SWAMP?... HOW COME THEY GOT AUTO-MOBILES WHILE WE GOT TO GET AROUND IN A RICKETY OL' FLAT-BOAT WIF A PUNKY NAME ON THE SIDE?
WHY JUST LOOK AT THIS MESSY OL' PLACE! LOOK AT THESE BORDERS! ...AIN'T EVEN DRAW'D WITH A RULER!
BY DAG... LE'S FACE IT! WE AIN' BIG TIME!
AFL UAW
SHH LI'L GRIM-DOOM

POLITICS AN' PARTIES? WHY MAN! WE BEEN FOOLIN' ROUN' WITH POLITICS AN' POLITICAL PARTIES FOR THE LONGEST TIME! ANIMALS COMIN' THROUGH THE SWAMP ALL THE TIME FOOLIN' ROUN' WITH POLITICS!
...YEAH! HOW 'BOUT THEM COWBIRDS SAYS THEY'RE DOVES?
...HOW 'BOUT THAT BIRD WATCHIN' MOLE?
WPA PWA

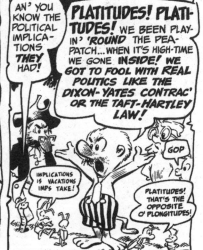

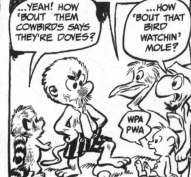

...OH, GOPO! PLEASE DON' GO MESSIN' ROUN' WITH POLITICS! DON' GO LOOKIN' FOR TROUBLE!
DON' HAVE TO GO LOOKIN'! IT RIGHT HERE IN THE SWAMP!
I BEEN KEEPIN' MY EYEBALLS PEELED! WE GOT THE REAL 100% McCOY POLITICS RIGHT HERE?... TAKE FOR EZZAMPLE THAT OL' WILDCAT HANGIN' OUT 'ROUND HERE...
GOPO
LSS NFS
...I SUPPOSEN'T YOU DON' KNOW WHO HE IS!... I SUPPOSEN'T YOU DON' REKKONIZE THEM HEAVY EYEBROWS... THE DARK EYELASHES AN' THE 7 O'CLOCK SHADOW!
YOU TALKIN' ABOUT OL' SIMPLE J. BALONEY?
...THAT SIMPLE J. BALONEY IS JES' A LOT O' MALARKEY! ...HE AIN'T NO BALONEY! ...HE REAL NAME IS McCARTHY!
B.O.
AN' THERE HE BE NOW!
3

BY JING... YOU RIGHT, GOPO! ...HE LOOK ZACKLY LIKE McCARTHY!
WE BEEN FLIM-FLAMMED!
QUEEG
How you hurt your elbow, bwah?
...WHY FROM SHAKIN' HANDS! YESSIR, I WAS SO NERVOUS AND MY HANDS WAS SHAKIN' SO THAT I MISSED HIM WITH THE FIST BUT CAUGHT HIM WITH THE ELBOW!
WE'LL GET UP A PETITION 'GAINST THAT OL' WILDCAT!
JOE MUS' GO!
Look like they don' like you, son!
...'COURSE THEY DON'T! THAT'S 'CAUSE I'M A UGLY OL' WILDCAT! OH WHY COULDN'TA I BEEN DRAWN A LOVEABLE LITTLE FLOPITTY RABBIT LIKE THEM!
...OR WHY COULDN' I EVEN HAVE SOME RESPECTABLE OLD-ENGLISH LETTERING LIKE YOU!
FDRJR

NOW HOL' ON EVERYBODY AFORE YOU GO A-HOOTIN' AND A-HOLLERIN' IT UP, I BEEN GIVIN' CAREFUL CONSIDERATION TO THIS WHOLE PROBLEM SINCE I BEEN LOOKIN' INTO POLITICS...
HST
PLEASE PLEASE GOPO! DON' GO MESSIN' ROUN' WITH POLITICS!

...AN' IT'S ALL VERY CLEAR TO ME THAT THE DOCTRINE OF STATES RIGHT EXPLAINS THIS WHOLE BLAMED THING! AS ANY FOOL CAN SEE, THE STATE LIKE THE INDIVIDUAL RESERVES SOVEREIGNTY...
SPLOOSH!
Potrzebie
SEWER OUTLET

...TO A CERTAIN DEGREE, AN' AS A RESULT IS INDEPENDENT OF FEDERAL LAW IN SOME CIRCUM-STANCES WHICH BRINGS ME TO MY MAIN POINT WHICH IS...
...IT WAS PUFFIKLY LEGAL TO FIRE ON FORT SUMTER!
SPCA
BY JING THAT'S THE TRUTH!
TELL 'EM, GOPO!

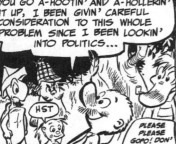

NOW DON'T GET CUTE! DON'T... DON'T GET CUTE WITH ME! IT'S VERY CLEAR WHAT YOU'RE UP TO!... IT'S VERY CLEAR THAT BY GETTING CUTE, BY FALLING IN WATER, ETC., AND ACTING CUTE, YOU SNEAK ACROSS YOUR SENILE IDEAS...
ZWICKR
... TALKS JES' LIKE BOB AN' RAY!
YOU DON'T FOOL ME!... YOU DON'T FOOL ME FOR A MINUTE! YOU'RE ALL DEMOCRATS! YOU DON'T FOOL ME, MISTER!
NAME CALLING! NAME CALLING!
...OH NO! OH NO DON'T PULL THAT ON ME!... YOU'RE ALL A BUNCH OF SOUTHERNERS! IT'S PLAIN BY YOUR ACCENTS YOU'RE A BUNCH OF SOUTHERNERS! A BUNCH OF SOLID-SOUTH DEMOCRATS! SENILE DEMOCRATS!
DIS-RE-SPECT!
DIS-RESPECT!
CENSURE! CENSURE!
BOY WHAT GOOD DRAWING! NOT LIKE COMIC-BOOK TRASH!
CIA
4

Hol' on, men! Ain't you read the papers last election? ...Ain't no more solid south! You is split wide open!
HE TALK MIGHTY FINE!
AIN'T IT GRAND THE WAY THE LETTERING IS!
RIGHT! ALL REPUBLI-CANS OVER HERE, BY DANG!
10,000,000 U.S. RED-BLOOD-ED BOYS FOR McCARTHY! SIGN PETITIONS!
TVA
AIN' BUT 3 DOZEN IN THE WHOLE SWAMP!
...Then again... all this foolishness done bust the Republican party wide open too!
HOORAW!!
SAY IT PURTY, MAN!
SNAP THEM GALUSES!
LIBERAL REPUB-LICANS BACK! BACK!
INDEPENDENTS TOO!
PLEASE! EVERYBODY PLEASE DON' GO MESSIN' ROUN' WITH POLITICS!
VEEP

...Then there's the talk about third party!
AAAHAAAA!
BY NEDDY-DINGO! THIRD PARTY! OVER HERE!
SONCHAKANNONDA!
PARTY GOING TO CAMP NIT-GE-DI-GET... OVER HERE!
NITGEDIGET
PDQ
HOOP! HOOP! WE IS BUSTED INTO A MESS O' PARTIES!
RIGHT! ...EACH PARTY GOT ONE MEMBER!
MY PARTY DOUBLED! WE GET TWO MEMBERS!
AN' MY PARTY'S THE BEST!
DOA
NO MINE!
MINE!
WAIT! YOU AIN'T HEARD THE WORST!

YOU AIN'T HEARD ALL WHAT'S BEEN GOIN' ON IN THE SWAMP!
...I SUPPOSENT YOU DON' REKKONIZE WHO ALPHONSE ALLIGATOR LOOK LIKE!
BY DING! IT AKCHOOLY WINSTON CHURCH-MOUSE!
NATO
WE IS INFIL-TRATED WITH THEM CARICATURES!
...AN' I SUPPOSENT YOU DON' REKKONIZE WHO TIDELAND OWL LOOK LIKE!
BY DONG! IT MARSH-LAND TITO!
IWW
HIM TOO! I THOUGHT HE BEHIN' THE OL' IRON WINDOW-SHADE!
...AN' I SUPPOSENT YOU DON' REKKONIZE WHO OL' TORTOISE LOOK LIKE!
BY KLINK! IT MENDUP FRANCE!
.4
MILK
5

...AN' OL' CORKY PORCUPINE IS WATERHOLE NEHRU!
UNESCO
...AN' OL' BLOOD-HOUND IS CHANGE-KI-CHECK!
AVG
...AN' YOUNG RACKLEDY COON IS CHEW-AN-PLAY!
...AN MOUSE IS GEORGIA MELLON-COUGH!
CCCP

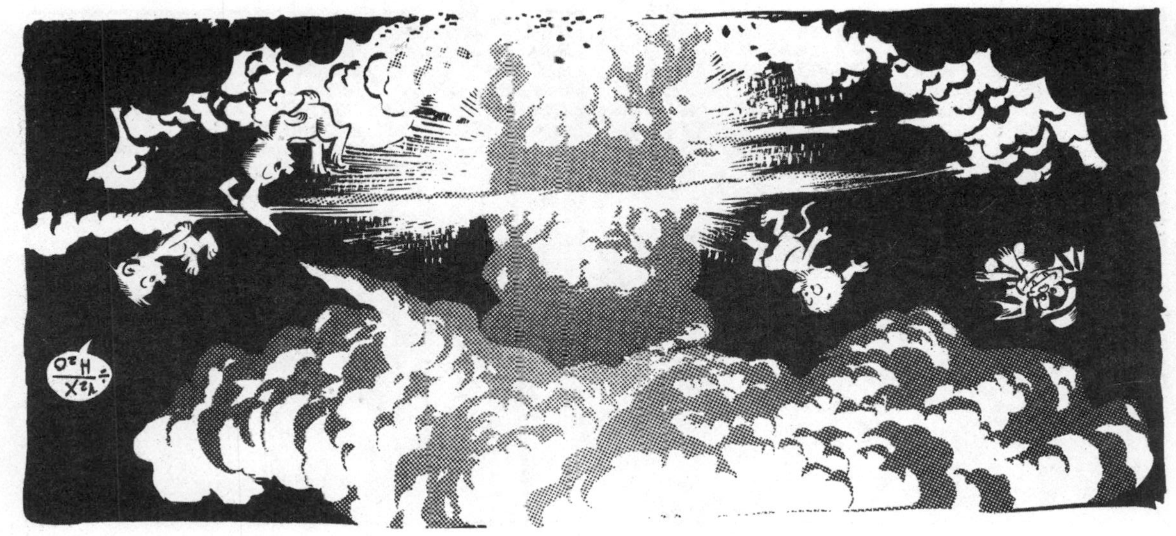
$\div \frac{\frac{1}{2}X}{H_2O}$

MY GOODNESS! LOOK OUT THERE! ISN'T THAT WHERE OUR COUSINS LIVE IN THE OKEEKEEFOONIE SWAMP?
I THINK IT IS! WHAT IN HEAVEN'S NAME COULD HAVE HAPPENED?
I TOL' 'EM NOT TO MESS AROUN'... *Puff*... AND NOW THEY GONE... *Puff*... THEY DONE BLOWED EACH OTHER UP... *Puff*... AND IT ALL **YOUR** FAULT... *Puff*! **YOU** TOL' GOPO WE COULD BE POPULAR AN' SUCCESSFUL LIKE YOU IF WE LEARNED **POLITICS** AND **JOINED A PARTY** YOU SAID!
UGH! UH!
LEARN **POLITICS** AND JOIN A **PARTY**? MERCY NO! THAT'S THE **KISS OF DEATH!** WE DIDN'T TELL HIM THAT!
WE TOLD HIM TO LEARN **PARLOR-TRICKS** AND JOIN A PARTY!... WHAT BETTER WAY CAN YOU BECOME POPULAR THEN BY GOING TO PARTIES AND DOING PARLOR TRICKS?
IT'S DARNOLD DUCK'S FAULT! IT'S A WONDER **ANYBODY** CAN UNDER-STAND HIM WHEN HE TALKS!
TSK TSK! ALL THE SWAMP FOLKS GONE! AN' IT WAS SUCH GOOD DRAWING TOO!
6

PUZZLE PAGE!

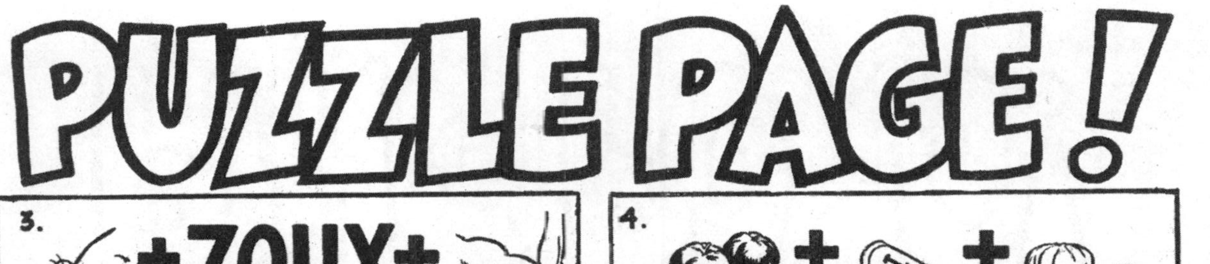

3.

+ZQUX+

–zqux–

+I=

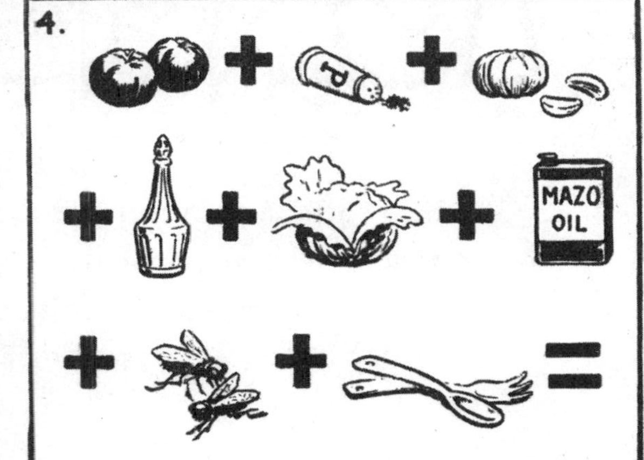

4.

ANSWERS ON LAST PAGE!

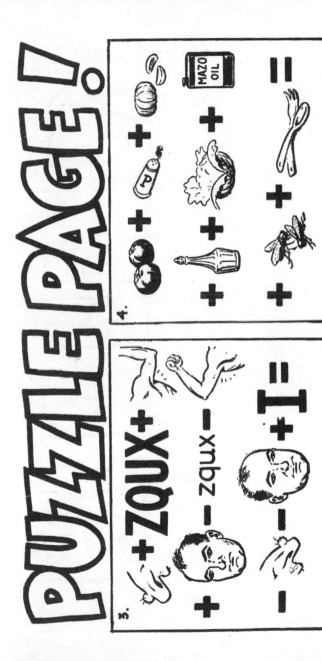

The tale was told by an old seafaring man, babbling in delirium before he died! Babbling amongst the flotsam and jetsam tossed upon the Coney Island shore he babbled . . . about a mysterious island in the tropics . . . about the lost tribe of the Ookabolaponga . . . about their god . . .

BILL ELDER
PTOO!
BOOM!
PUFFED RICE
POST NO BILLS
THIS IS NOT A 3-D MOVIE! THIS IS DEFINITELY IT!

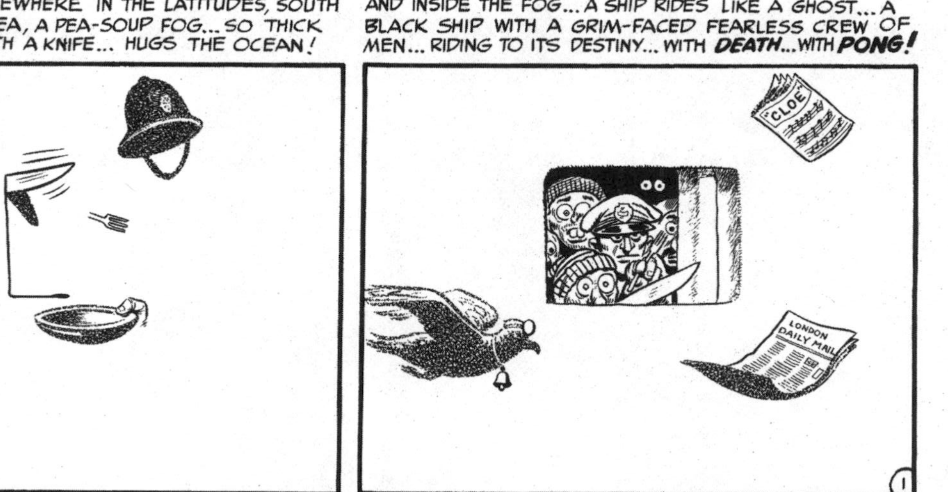
THE TROPICS!... SOMEWHERE IN THE LATITUDES, SOUTH OF THE SARGOSSA SEA, A PEA-SOUP FOG... SO THICK YOU COULD CUT IT WITH A KNIFE... HUGS THE OCEAN!
AND INSIDE THE FOG... A SHIP RIDES LIKE A GHOST... A BLACK SHIP WITH A GRIM-FACED FEARLESS CREW OF MEN... RIDING TO ITS DESTINY... WITH DEATH... WITH PONG!
CLOE
LONDON DAILY MAIL
1

MM! JUST TASTE THIS FOG! DELI-CIOUS PEA-SOUP!
WE'LL **NEVER** FIND THE ISLAND OF THE FEROCIOUS OOKABOLA-PONGA!
WAIT! THE FOG IS LIFTING! NOW WE'LL KNOW WHAT PART OF THE OCEAN WE'RE IN!
PORT SIDE
TRAMP & HOBO STEAMER
NO RELATION TO STANLEY
LOOK! WE'RE NOT IN THE OCEAN! WE'VE BEEN SAILING ON **LAND!** WE'RE **LOST!**
EVERYBODY LOOK AROUND FOR SOME RECOGNIZABLE LANDMARK!
CAW!
CAW!
CAW!
ALBANY OR BUST
S.S. H.M.S. N.R.A.P.S.

I, CECIL B.V.D. MILL, MOVIE PRODUCER, WHO HAS CHARTERED THIS SHIP TO MAKE A MOVIE AMIDST THE SAVAGE OOKABOLA-PONGA, SHALL LOOK FOR LANDMARKS!
YES, B.V.D.!
I, CAPTAIN OF SHIP CHARTERED BY B.V.D., THIRTY Y'ARS BEFORE THE MAST, MAN AND BOY... AM BEST LAND-MARK SPOTTER ON SEVEN SEAS!
WE, HEARTY AND BRAVE CREW OF SHIP... ALWAYS EFFICIENT AND ON THE JOB, SHALL HELP CAPTAIN LOOK FOR LANDMARKS!
DEATH
I, LANA LYNN, BIG SHOT LEADING LADY FOR THIS FILM, DO NOT UNDER-STAND, WHY YOU ALL LOOK THIS-A WAY WHEN LANDMARKS ARE ALL THAT-A WAY!
ART OF JUI-JITSU
STAR-BOARD SIDE. (GET IT?)

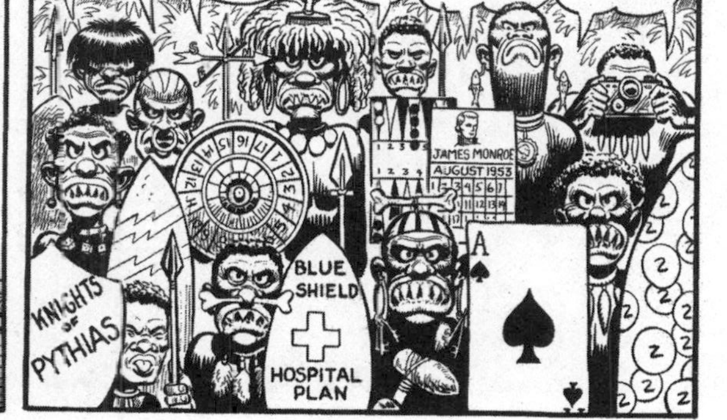
CAPTAIN, MY CAPTAIN!... LOOK!... OUT THERE!... ON THE STARBOARD LARBOARD! ... S-STREAMING OUT OF THE J-J-JUNGLE! ... THE OO...OO...OO-OO...OO-OO-OO...
BVD
ZIP
LIFE SAVERS
...THE OOKABOLAPONGA!
...HUGGA BUGGA...
HUGGA BUGGA...
HUGGA BUGGA...
HUGGA BUGGA...
HUGGA BUGGA...
JAMES MONROE
AUGUST 1953
KNIGHTS OF PYTHIAS
BLUE SHIELD
HOSPITAL PLAN

CAPTAIN! IT'S THE FEROCIOUS OOKA-BOLAPONGA! CAN YOU SPEAK TO THEM?
THE FEROCIOUS OOKABOLAPONGA SPEAK A STRANGE WILD TONGUE THAT IS HEARD NOWHERE ELSE ON EARTH... BUT I WILL TRY!
...TIYO KIMOSAVEE OOKA-BOLAPONGA! VAS MACHST DU, KID? OWHAY ISAY ISNESSBAY?
MP
ONE WAY
PARIS
ENGLAND
ROM
SPAIN
LEVITTOWN
ISNESSBAY OULDCAY EBAY ETTERBAY! OUYAY OW-KNAY OWHAY ITAY ISAY! OUYAY OTGAY OOTAY IPSHAY ALOTAY!
IDDAY OUYAY EESAY ETHAY ATESTLAY ISSUEAY OFAY 'ADMAY'?
GOOD NEWS, B.V.D.! I CAN COMMUNICATE WITH THEM!
OUYAY ETBAY! ITAY ASWAY 'EORGEGAY'!
B.V.D.
BVD
HI-FLYER

I SAY! YOU FELLOWS SPEAK ENGLISH?... WHY DIDN'T YOU SAY SO IN THE FIRST PLACE!
FOR A MOMENT I THOUGHT YOU ONLY SPOKE THAT FILTHY OOKABOLAPONGANESE! HORRIBLE LANGUAGE TO MASTER! NEVER DID TAKE TO IT!
KEEP OFF THE GRASS

...HEY! WHAT YOU GOT? GOOD LOOKIN' DOLL? HOWZABOUT TRADE FOR HER?
HMPH! QUAINT PEASANTS! PROBABLY WANT TO SWAP YOU FOR SOME HAND-MADE POTS AND TRINKETS!
...NO! DIS MY LEADING LADY! ME NO TRADE!
OFF LIMITS

COME ON! WE NEED WOMAN FOR SACRIFICE! WE TRADE! I GOT BUBBLE-GUM TICKETS OF WHOLE BROOKLYN DODGER BASE-BALL TEAM... AND TICKETS OF INDIAN TRIBES OF WILD WEST! WE TRADE, HUH?
YOU'VE GOT THE **WHOLE TEAM?**

WHAT A TRADE! FOR YEARS I'VE BEEN TRYING TO GET THE BUBBLE-GUM TICKETS OF PEE-WEE REESE AND EDDIE STANKY! NOW MY COLLECTION IS COMPLETE!
HUGGA BUGGA...HUGGA BUGGA...
ADVICE FOR THIN PEOPLE- DON'T EAT FAST!! ADVICE FOR FAT PEOPLE- DON'T EAT— FAST!!
HOT DOG! I CAN SEE IT NOW IN LIGHTS! "B.V.D. MILL PRESENTS... ACTUAL PICTURES OF HUMAN SACRIFICE!" SET UP THE CAMERA RIGHT THERE ON THAT HUGE TOE-NAIL SHAPED ROCK!
... THE TOE-NAIL SHAPED ROCK ON THIS FOOT-SHAPED HILL CONNECTED TO THIS LEG SHA... SHA... SHA... SHA...
HUGGA BUGGA
YES, B.V.D.!
HUGGA BUGGA
HUGGA BUGGA
3

Post writers in the sky
PONG!
BOING
BING
BONG
BOP
BIP
IT'S ALL RIGHT MEN! STAND YOUR GROUND MEN! DON'T SHOW HIM YOU'RE SCARED!
BVD

PING PONG!
HUGGA BUGGA!
GET OUT THE WAY!
NO SPEAK ENGLISH!
HEAD FOR THE SHIP!
SUBWAY GUARD

TO HECK WITH THE SHIP!
IT'S TOO SLOW!
I'M GOING HOME! AIN'T NUTHIN' CAN STOP ME!
NOTHING?
SQUEE
SUDDENLY, WE CHANGE OUR MINDS!
WE GO BACK!
AFTER ALL, I FORGOT TO PUT MY RUBBERS ON!
WE DELIVER ANYWHERE

O.K., MEN! WE'RE HERE TO MAKE A MOVIE! AND LANA LYNN, MY LEADING LADY, HAS BEEN KIDNAPPED BY A HORRIBLE MONSTER! IT IS OUR DUTY TO FOLLOW IT INTO THE JUNGLE AND RESCUE HER!
IF ANY OF YOU ARE (**HAH**)... **SCARED** TO GO... YOU MAY STEP OUT OVER HERE!
FOOOOOM
O.K.! HALF GOES AND HALF STAYS TO WATCH THE SHIP!
NOW, IF WE COULD ONLY FIND SOME FOOTPRINTS TO FOLLOW!
ANYONE SEE FOOTPRINTS?
PICNIC AREA
4

SINCE WE SEE NO FOOTPRINTS, WE'LL HAVE TO FOLLOW THIS STREAM ON THIS RAFT! LOOK!... IT GOES INTO THAT CAVE UP AHEAD!
ROBERT HALL LOW OVERHEAD
TUNNEL OF LOVE
MY GOSH!... A PREHISTORIC *DIPLODOCUS BRONTOSAURUS!* *WHAT A SCENE! QUICK, MAN! GET A SHOT OF THAT!*
YES, B.V.D.!
P.A.L.
CHOMPF!

LOOK! OVER THERE! A TYRRANOSAURUS STEGOSAURUS FRAMMIS! QUICK! GET A SHOT OF IT, YOU FOOL!
YES, B.V.D.!
LOOK! LOOK! AN ARCHAEOPTERYX IKTHEPOSAURUS RAZZLE-DAZZLEBUS PTERODACTYL PTOOEY! GET A SHOT!
YES, B.V.D.!
BEGIN MEASURED MILE
LOOK! LOOKLOOK! A JUSTPLAINTSAURUS! GET A SHOT OF THAT, LAD!
YES, B.V.D.!
WURF!
END OF MEASURED MILE
JOE STALIN SLEPT HERE

TRY TO GET AN INSIDE SHOT OF THAT JUSTPLAINTSAURUS, BO!
FILTHY LUCK, CAPTAIN! ONLY TWO OF US LEFT!
URP!
YES, B.V.D.!
ABSOLUTELY LAST CHANCE GAS STATION!
SPEARMINT
DRIVE-IN
WE'LL BE ABLE TO GET A GOOD VIEW FROM THIS HILL! LOOK! OVER THERE!
A HUGE MOUNTAIN, CARVED BY THE NEVER-ENDING WIND BY SOME STRANGE COINCI-DENCE INTO A CRUDE SHAPE VAGUELY RESEMBLING A... A... A...
...A CIGARETTE LIGHTER I ONCE HAD!
10¢
NO SPITTING
5

COME ON, CAPTAIN! THAT'S PING PONG'S HIDEAWAY! I'VE PAID YOU MILLIONS FOR THIS VOYAGE AND WE'RE GOING UP THERE!
...BUT B.V.D.! I'M TIRED! I CAN'T GO ON MUCH LONGER! I'LL NEVER MAKE IT TO THAT MOUNTAIN! I'M TIRED, BOY!
B.V.D
BVD
ROCK & RYE
BAH! SIXTY-POUND WEAKLING! LETTING A LITTLE MOUNTAIN TIRE YOU OUT! C'MON, LAD! WE'RE ALMOST TO THE ENTRANCE ON TOP! **MUSH,** BOY, **MUSH!**
PLANETARIUM
UGH!... OPENING... JUST A FEW MORE FEET... LISTEN... HORRIBLE SHRIEKS...
...WHAT IS MONSTER... UGH... DOING... TO LANA... LYNN...
L-L-LOOK!
HOW TO AVOID BEING DRAFTED
YOW!
OW
EEE

EEK... EE...OO...
OI... FILTHY BEAST! DON'T TOUCH ME!
POW
SPLAT
SPLAT

OWOO...
EEE... HELP!
HOW DARE YOU TOUCH ME, YOU... YOU...BIG APE!
PAF
-IN THE LABONZA-
-IN THE LABONZA
!!!

IT'S BEEN HOURS SINCE B.V.D. AND THE OTHER HALF OF THE CREW WENT INTO THE JUNGLE AFTER PING PONG!
LISTEN! DO YOU HEAR FOOTSTEPS!
TROMP
TROMP
TROMP
WE'RE NOT AFRAID! ARE WE, MEN?
25¢ AN HOUR BRONX PARK BOAT HOUSE
YOU BET WE ARE!
COME BACK, MEN! IT'S O.K.! WE'VE GOT PING PONG UNDER CONTROL!
ZAP
TROMP
TROMP
6

B.V.D.! HERE WE ARE... NO ROOM ON THE SHIP... HAD TO GET RID OF THE CREW... ADRIFT... NO FOOD... NO WATER... WHAT I WANT TO KNOW IS, WAS THIS TRIP NECESSARY?
CAPTAIN! I'M GOING TO GET PING PONG BACK TO BROADWAY EVEN IF IT **KILLS** YOU! WHICH GIVES ME A GOOD IDEA, MAINLY SINCE I'M GETTING **HUNGRY**!
CLICK
"THE VULGAR BOATMAN"
WAIT A MINUTE, B.V.D.!... LOOKY OVER YONDER... ***IT'S LAND!... IT'S NEW YORK!***

I MADE IT! I MADE IT! GLORY BE... YEAH MAN... YOU KNOW THE SPECTACULAR FILM WITH A CAST OF THOUSANDS IN GLORIOUS TECHNICOLOR CALLED CROW VADIS? WELL I MADE IT!
GAINES INSURANCE CO. "IF YOU LOSE AN ARM WE HELP YOU LOOK FOR IT!"
LOOK EVERYBODY! I, B.V.D. MILL, HAVE COME BACK WITH THIS STUPENDOUS MONSTER... HEY, EVERYBODY?
...HEY?... ISN'T ANYBODY INTERESTED, HEY? DOESN'T ANYONE WANT TO LOOK AT THIS COLOSSAL MONSTER?
...HEY?
JUST OUT! THE SENSATIONAL, GREAT, TERRIFIC, AMAZING NEW CLEANSER "SOAP!"

SEE! IT ALL GOES TO SHOW, CAPTAIN!
IN THIS HIGH SPEED CIVILIZATION, NOTHING SURPRISES ANYONE ANY MORE!
Mother come home-
WE Found your
Latest issue
of MAD!
MAD
7

PUZZLE PAGE!
5.
6.
ANSWERS ON LAST PAGE!

One thing that gets us about the cartoon world is . . . you have these strong guys! . . No matter what happens . . . no matter how bad things are . . . no matter what . . . who . . . how . . . who . . . who . . . how . . . ha . . . who . . . ha . . . who . . . who-ha. . . . These guys wind up being the strongest! . . . Like forinstance . . . take this guy . .

THIMBLE
THIMBLE THEATRE
NOW PLAYING "SEW BIG" A NEW YARN BY EDNA FABRIC
NOW MAZOLA OIL, HONEY... THAT'S NO REASON TO GET MAD AT ME JUST BECAUSE I YAM A SQUINTY-EYED SAILOR!
LIMBURGERS
YOU'RE A SQUINTY-EYED SAILOR, ALL RIGHT... WHEN THE PRETTY GIRLS PASS BY YOU ALL OF A SUDDEN GET SQUINTY-EYED! OTHERWISE A REGULAR EYED SAILOR!
THE GREASY 'FLY' CHOP HOUSE.
APPROVED BY DEPT. OF SANITATION
HAMBURGERS.
TROMP
TROMP
MU 3-5445
MU 3-5445
MU 3-5445
Elder

I YAM SURPRISED AT YOU, MAZOLA! DON'T YOU KNOW IT AIN'T NICE TO TROMP ME WITH YOUR SHOES?
...I YAM IN LUCK! I HAVE IN THE BOTTOM OF MY POCKET, SOME OLD STEWED **SPINACH!**
OOH! FOR SOME SPINACH!
TROMP TROMP TROMP TROMP
CHOMP CHOMP CHOMP GULP
SWISS NAVY
TOOT!
POP!
DANCLANG!
...LIKE I WUZ SAYING...IT AIN'T NICE TO TROMP WITH YOUR SHOES!...YOU GOTTA TAKE YOUR SHOES OFF FIRST!
...WHEW! THAT WAS A NARROW ES-CAPE!...LUCKY I HAPPENED TO HAVE THAT STEWED SPINACH!
SWISS
TROMP TROMP
NOTE: BARNACLES

HOWEVER... EVEN WITHOUT SHOES... THE ODD CLUB-LIKE SHAPE OF MY FORELEGS ENABLE ME TO DELIVER CRUSHING TROMPS!
HARK!... I THINK I YAM HEARING SWEE'BACK CRYING IN THE BACKGROUND!
WAA
TROMP TROMP
TROMPITTY TROMP
SWEE'BACK! SWEE'BACK! WHAT HAPPENED?
... NOW, POOPEYE, DON'T GET EXCITED! BABIES CRY FOR SIMPLE REASONS... LIKE WHEN THEY'RE TEETHING... THE TEETH PUSHING THROUGH IRRITATE THEM!... POOR 'ITTLE SWEE'BACK IS 'OO CRYING CAUSE GUMS HURT... 'CAUSE TOOTH IS COMING OUT?
... DAT'S WIGHT, AUNT MAZOLA! I YAM CRYING 'CAUSE TOOTH YAM COMING OUT!... WAY, WAY OUT!... WAY WAY WAY OUT... INTO MY HAND!
THERE'S SOME SAILOR IN EVERY PORT— &-SOME PORT IN EVERY SAILOR!

...BUT YAM NOT COMING OUT 'CAUSE I YAM TEETHING... YAM COMING OUT BECAUSE THAT OLD LADY GAVE ME A BELT IN THE KISSER!
BECAUSE I BELIEVE IN FAIR PLAY, I'M GOING TO SOCK HER!... BECAUSE I BELIEVE IN JUSTICE, I'M GOING TO SOCK HER!... BUT MAINLY BECAUSE SHE'S AN OLD LADY AND CAN'T HIT BACK... I'M GOING TO SOCK HER!
POP
AN OLD LADY BY NAME OF...
...BY NAME OF...
MM-CAT-BURGER
...BY NAME OF MAMMY JOKEUM!
GONNG

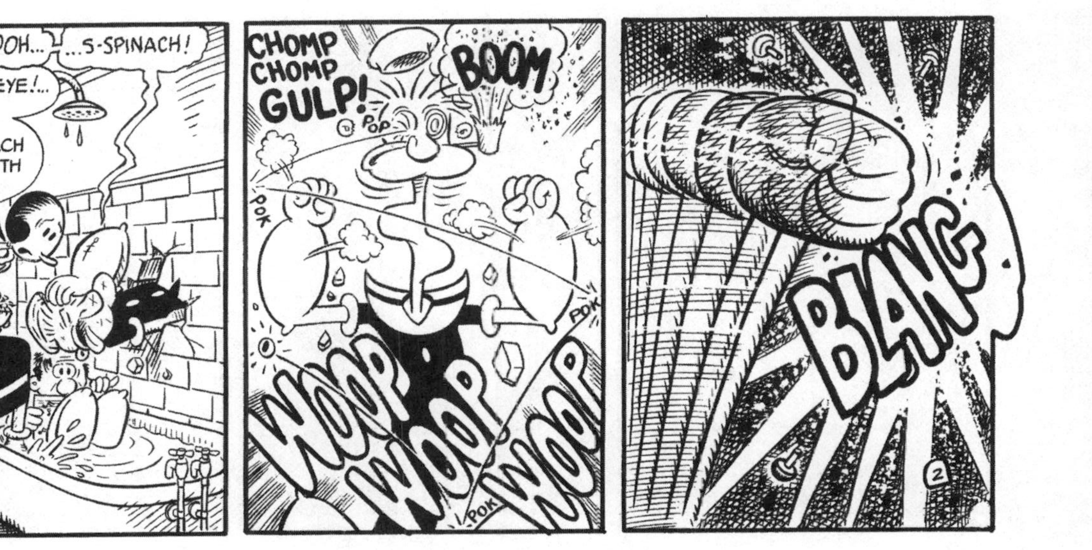
SPINACH... OOOH... ...S-SPINACH!
HERE, POOPEYE!... A BOWL OF MARINATED PICKLED SPINACH SPRINKLED WITH EXTRA-FINE SAND!
CHOMP CHOMP GULP!
POP
BOOM
POK
POK
WOOP WOOP WOOP
POK
BLANG

...THAT'LL TEACH YOU NOT TO HIT SWEE'BACK AGAIN!
IF THERE'S ANYTHING I CAN'T STAND, IT'S TO SEE ANYONE PUSH SOMEONE WEAKER THAN THEM-SELVES AROUND!
GIVE BLOOD HERE!
...UH-OH! HERE COMES HER SON!
S.S. KON TIKI
I SUPPOSE YOU COME TO GET WHO HIT ME, YOUR MAMMY, EH SON? ...WELL THERE'S THE ONE WHO HIT ME... THE ONE WITH THE SAILOR HAT!...GO GIVE THAT POOPEYE A GOOD SHOT IN THE HEAD!
THE NEW CHRISTIAN DIOR FORM
HEH HEH! LITTLE DOES HE KNOW THAT THE ONE WITH THE SAILOR HAT IS IN REALITY MAMMY!... BY GEORGE... I'VE ALWAYS SUSPECTED WE LOOKED ALIKE!
POW
CRAK
UH-OH!... I THINK I YAM AGAIN HEARING SWEE'BACK CRYING IN THE BACKGROUND!
BIF
SOK
WAA

SWEE'BACK! SWEE'BACK! WHAT HAPPENED THIS TIME?
...NOW POOPEYE, DON'T GET EXCITED! BABIES CRY FOR ALL KINDS OF SIMPLE REASONS! POOR 'ITTLE SWEE'BACK! IS 'OO CRYING 'CAUSE MAYBE DIAPER PIN OPENED AND IS STICKING 'OO?
...LET AUNT MAZOLA TAKE A LOOK!
JUMBO BURGER..
HOW DRY I YAM
MADAME, TAKE YOUR COTTON PICKIN' HANDS OFFEN MY DIAPER!
...BY GEORGE IT'S FANTASTIC HOW THE MINUTE THESE CHARACTERS GET INTO A COMIC BOOK, THEY START ACTING IN BAD TASTE!
BURGER-MEISTER..

BUT I YAM NOT CRYING 'CAUSE DIAPER PIN IS STICK-ING ME! I YAM CRYING 'CAUSE THAT OLD MAN ON THE RIGHT GAVE ME A BELT IN THE KISSER... THE FAR RIGHT!
...AND SO, ONCE MORE, BECAUSE I BELIEVE IN AN EYE FOR AN EYE... A KISSER FOR A KISSER... AND MAINLY 'CAUSE OLD PEOPLE ARE EASIEST TO FIGHT... I ATTACK!
HELP SUPPORT B.O.B.O.
AH YES... THE OLD MAN ON THE FAR-**FAR** RIGHT... "OLD MAN" BEING IN THE BRITISH VERNACULAR SUCH AS "OLD BOY"... "OLD CHAP," ETC... NOT NECECERRILY CONNOTING "OLD" IN THE DIRECT SENSE...
...YES... THE OLD MAN BY NAME OF **MELVIN OF THE APES!**
POP!
HELP SUPPORT THE PHILADELPHIA ATHLETICS.
3

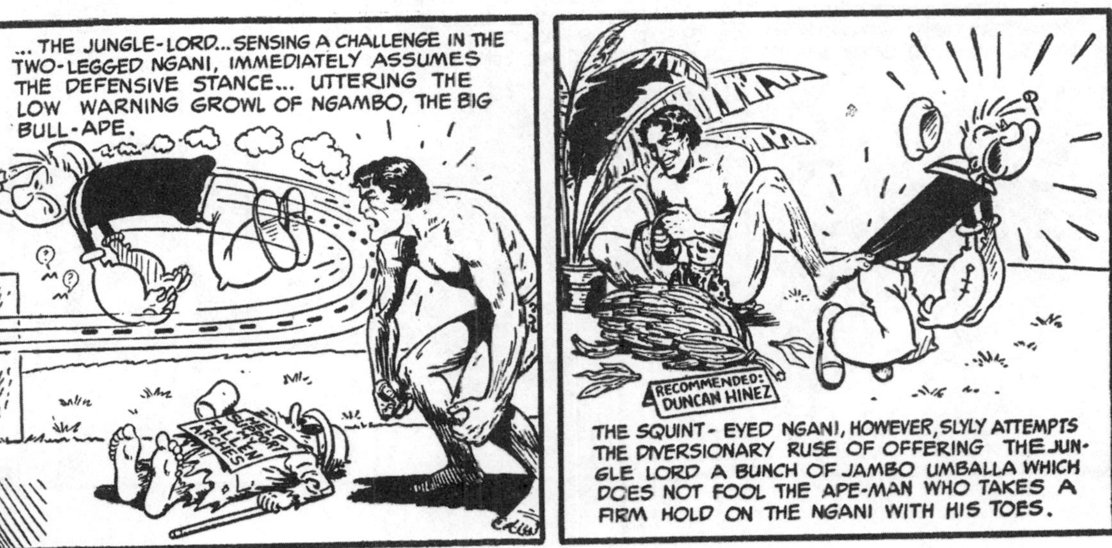

... THE JUNGLE-LORD... SENSING A CHALLENGE IN THE TWO-LEGGED NGANI, IMMEDIATELY ASSUMES THE DEFENSIVE STANCE... UTTERING THE LOW WARNING GROWL OF NGAMBO, THE BIG BULL-APE.
HELP SUPPORT MY FALLEN ARCHES
RECOMMENDED: DUNCAN HINEZ
THE SQUINT-EYED NGANI, HOWEVER, SLYLY ATTEMPTS THE DIVERSIONARY RUSE OF OFFERING THE JUNGLE LORD A BUNCH OF JAMBO UMBALLA WHICH DOES NOT FOOL THE APE-MAN WHO TAKES A FIRM HOLD ON THE NGANI WITH HIS TOES.

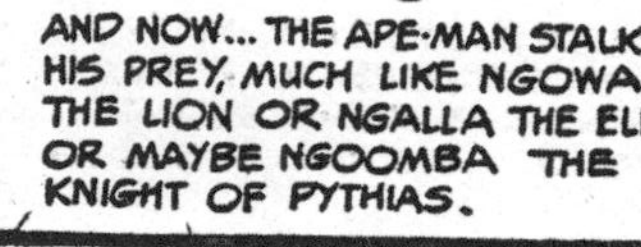
AND NOW... THE APE-MAN STALKS HIS PREY, MUCH LIKE NGOWA THE LION OR NGALLA THE ELK OR MAYBE NGOOMBA THE KNIGHT OF PYTHIAS.

SHICK
WASSERMAN
TYPHOID
BOOBONIC PLAGUE
...SUDDENLY, THE JUNGLE LORD LEAPS... HIS SINEWY ARMS CLOSING LIKE STEEL BANDS... MUSCLES TENSING, STRAINING, BULGING, TILL A LOUD "CRACK" IS HEARD...

...FOR MELVIN OF THE APES HAS A SICKENING HABIT OF CRACKING HIS KNUCKLES ALL THE TIME! ...THEN WITH HIS KNUCKLES AUSGECRACKED... BACK TO THE ATTACK.

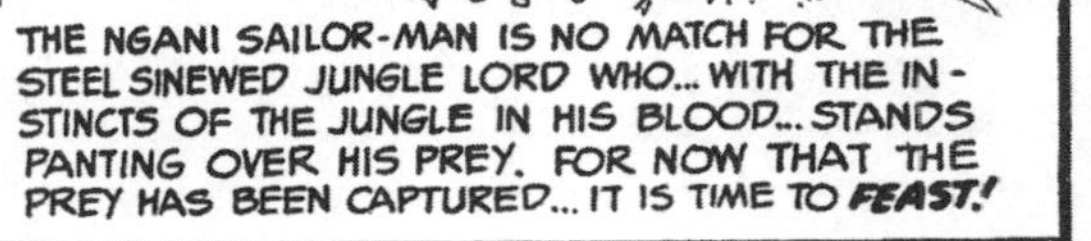
THE NGANI SAILOR-MAN IS NO MATCH FOR THE STEEL SINEWED JUNGLE LORD WHO... WITH THE IN-STINCTS OF THE JUNGLE IN HIS BLOOD... STANDS PANTING OVER HIS PREY. FOR NOW THAT THE PREY HAS BEEN CAPTURED... IT IS TIME TO FEAST!

FOR NOW IT IS NGMELVIN THE BULL-APE GIVING THE BLOOD CURDLING CRY OF VICTORY BEFORE THE FEAST! ...EYES GLEAMING, FANGS BARED, THE APE-MAN CROU-CHES TO FEAST...AND SO, HE EATS HIS SWISS CHEESE ON WHITE BREAD SANDWICH THAT JANE HAS WRAPPED FOR HIM.
4

SPINACH! OOH... SPINACH!
...HERE, POOPEYE!...A PLATE OF SPINACH PIZZA-PIE WITH PARMESAN CHEEZE AND GROUND-GLASS GRIT!
CHOMP CHOMP CHOMP GULP
TSSSS BOOM
RAT TAT TAT TAT TAT TAT

AS USUAL, MAZOLA...YOU BROUGHT THAT SPINACH IN THE NICK OF TIME!... THAT'LL TEACH THAT MELVIN OF THE APES NOT TO HIT SWEE'BACK AGAIN!
...YAAH... COME ON DOWN, MELVIN, AND FIGHT LIKE A MAN... NOT LIKE AN APE!... THROWING COCONUTS... TSK... TSK... TSK!
CLOP
WAA
...UH-OH! SWEE'BACK IS CRYING AGAIN! ...SWEE'BACK!... SWEE'BACK! WO' HOPPEN?
...NOW POOPEYE! LIKE I SAID BEFORE, BABIES CRY FOR ALL SIMPLE KINDS REASONS!... POOR 'ITTLE SWEE'BACK... IS 'OO CRYING 'CAUSE MAYBE 'OO GOT BUBBLE INSIDE WHILE DRINKING FROM YOUR MILK BOTTLE?
...LET AUNT MAZOLA BUBBLE OO...
GIRL BURGER—

FAW CWYIN' OUT WOWD, AUNT MAZOLA! QUIT PATTING ME ON THE BACK, TRYING TO BELCH ME!... IF I WANT TO BELCH, I TAKE SELTZER!
... HOWEVER... TO GET BACK TO THE MAIN STORY LINE... REASON I AM CRYING IS... I HAVE BEEN AGAIN BELTED... THIS TIME, FOR VARIETY'S SAKE, NOT IN THE KISSER BUT IN THE DIAPER...
SMAK
SMESH
ZOK
... BY THAT MISERABLE EMACIATED LOOKING WRETCH OVER THERE BY NAME OF **CLARK BENT!**
ONCE MORE I GO TO FIGHT FOR LAW AND ORDER... FOR JUSTICE... BUT MAINLY FOR ADDING SADISTIC ELEMENT THAT IS SUCH A VITAL PART OF COMIC BOOKS!
KOF
HAK
KOF
GOPHER BURGER
KOF
HAK
KAF
KOF
SMEK
SMOK
SMIK
5

...BY GEORGE! I ACTUALLY KNOCKED HIM WITH-OUT ANY EXTRA SPINACH!
(KAFF) EXCUSE ME (GASP) WHILE I GO LOOK (HAK! HAK!) FOR CON-VENIENT PHONE BOOTH!
MONTGOMERY'S KOSHER HAMBURGER SHOPS.
HAK
KAF
KOF
...THERE HE GOES... INTO THAT PHONE BOOTH THAT JUST HAPPENS TO BE CONVENIENTLY LOCATED IN THE MIDDLE OF THE FOOTBALL FIELD NEARBY!
...THE PHONE BOOTH!...THAT NAME!...DO YOU KNOW WHO THAT STRANGER IS?
HAK-KOF
KOF
...WHY THAT'S... THAT'S THE LONE RAN-GER!
...OH NO!...IF IT WAS...THEN WHEN YOU SAID WHAT YOU JUST SAID... THE LONE RAN-GER WOULD JUMP ON HIS HORSE AND RIDE AWAY WITH THE WILLIAM TELL OVERTURE IN THE BACKGROUND!...I THINK THAT CLARK BENT IS IN REALITY, **SUPERDUPERMAN!**
PIG BURGER..

LOOK! HE'S COMING OUT OF THE PHONE BOOTH!
WE KNOW WHO YOU ARE!... TELL THE TRUTH, CLARK BENT... DIDN'T YOU GO INTO THAT CONVENIENT PHONE BOOTH TO CHANGE INTO YOUR TRUE IDENTITY OF SUPERDUPERMAN?
... BY GEORGE... IT'S A GOOD THING YOU REMINDED ME! I'D FORGOTTEN FOR A MINUTE THAT IN REALITY I WAS SUPERDUPERMAN!... LIKE A DOPE I BEEN SITTING IN THAT PHONE BOOTH MAKING A **PHONE CALL!**
YOU JUST WAIT THERE WHILE I DASH BACK INTO THIS PHONE BOOTH AND TAKE OFF MY COAT, SHIRT, BASKETBALL SHOES, SPATS, SWEAT-SOCKS, SWEATER, SWEAT-SHIRT, SWEAT, LONG JOHNS... **WOOPS!...** GOTTA PUT BACK THEM LONG JOHNS... THAT'S MY UNIFORM!
BREAD BOX
MAE BUSCH
ZIP

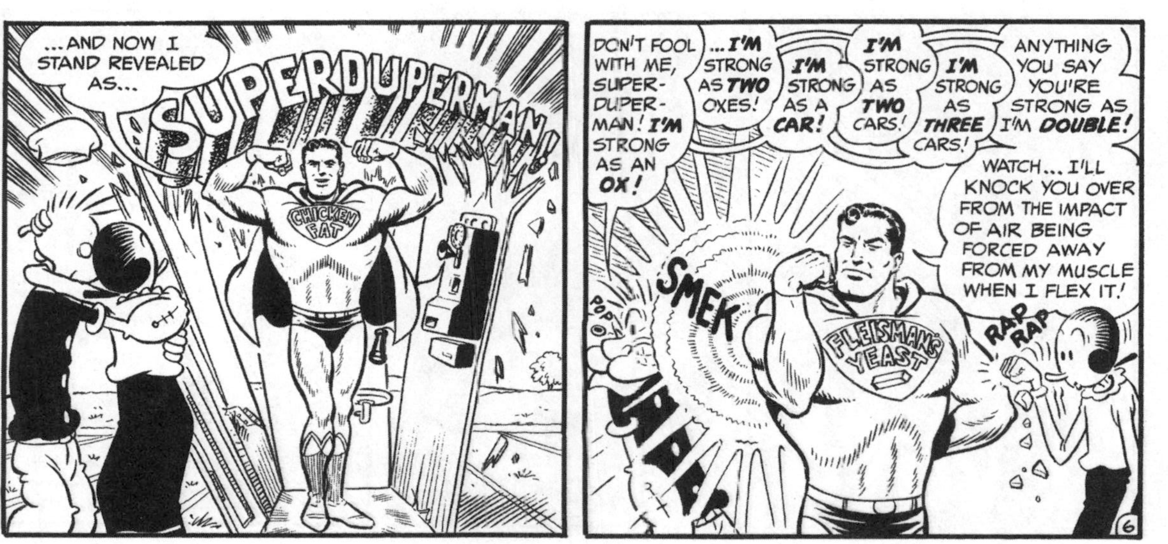
...AND NOW I STAND REVEALED AS...
SUPERDUPERMAN!
CHICKEN FAT
DON'T FOOL WITH ME, SUPER-DUPER-MAN! I'M STRONG AS AN OX!
...I'M STRONG AS TWO OXES!
I'M STRONG AS A CAR!
I'M STRONG AS TWO CARS!
I'M STRONG AS THREE CARS!
ANYTHING YOU SAY YOU'RE STRONG AS I'M DOUBLE!
WATCH... I'LL KNOCK YOU OVER FROM THE IMPACT OF AIR BEING FORCED AWAY FROM MY MUSCLE WHEN I FLEX IT!
SMEK
POP
FLEISMAN'S YEAST
RAP RAP
6

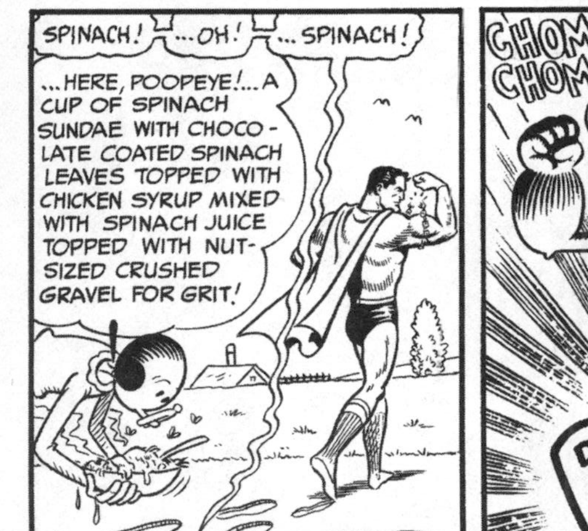
SPINACH! ...OH! ...SPINACH!
...HERE, POOPEYE!... A CUP OF SPINACH SUNDAE WITH CHOCO-LATE COATED SPINACH LEAVES TOPPED WITH CHICKEN SYRUP MIXED WITH SPINACH JUICE TOPPED WITH NUT-SIZED CRUSHED GRAVEL FOR GRIT!
CHOMP CHOMP GULP
BLOM
BLRASHHH

PLEASE DON'T HIT ME ANY MORE... P-PLEASE DON'T HIT ME!... I'LL GET OUT OF HERE FASTER THAN A SPEEDING BULLET!... I'LL LEAP OVER THE BUILDING AT A SINGLE BOUND! I'LL BOUNCE OUT OF HERE LIKE POTRZEBIE!
THAT'LL TEACH YOU NOT TO HIT SWEE'BACK!
OH, POOPEYE... FOR THE WAY YOU HAVE FOUGHT FOR ME ... FOR THE WAY YOU HAVE PROTECTED ME... I CAN ONLY EXPRESS MY FEELINGS TOWARDS YOU WITH ONE AFFECTIONATE EXPRESSION, ONE AFFECTIONATE WORD WHICH IS...
...SCHVIENHUNT!
PLASTIC DOLL
BOY...AM I EVER DISGUSTED! ...YOU AND YOUR FURSHLUGGINER SPINACH! I GUESS I'LL HAVE TO TAKE CARE OF YOU MYSELF!
...SWEE'BACK!...YOU STRUCK ME!... WHAT DOES THIS MEAN, KICKING ME IN THE BACK!... YOU HAVE HURT ME DEEPLY... NOT THE FLESH, BUT THE SOUL... ESPECIALLY SINCE I CARRY A RARE HIP-FLASK IN MY BACK POCKET!... I WARN YOU... DON'T KICK ME IN THE BACK AGAIN!
PHUD

BOY, IT'S A LUCKY THING FOR YOU, SWEE'BACK, THAT YOU'RE LISTENING TO MY WARNING AND NOT KICKING ME IN THE BACK! IT'S A LUCKY THING FOR YOU YOU'RE KICKING ME IN THE SHINS, BOY!
HERE, POOPEYE! I THINK YOU'LL NEED THIS LAST BIT OF SPINACH LEFT IN THE REFRIGERATOR!
FIRST OF ALL... CALL ME MISTER SWEE'BACK!... I'M NOT REALLY AN INFANT... I'M A MIDGET (AS IF AN INFANT COULD HAVE SUCH A DEVELOPED VOCABULARY)!
CALL FOR PHILIP MORRIS
KUF
...SECOND OF ALL... THOSE OTHER CHARACTERS WEREN'T HITTING ME AT ALL!... I WAS JUST TRYING TO TRICK YOU INTO GETTING A BEATING FROM ONE OF THEM SUPPOSEDLY INVINCIBLE BUMS!... HA!... I HOPE THEY GET FIRED WHEN THEY GO BACK TO THEIR COMIC-STRIPS!
...O.K. FOR YOU, SWEE'-BACK!...I'M EATING SPINACH, SWEE'BACK!... YOU'RE GOING TO GET IT IN THE LABONZA, SWEE'BACK...
PIDGEON-BURGER..
MORE BOUNCE TO THE OUNCE! 2¢ PLAIN
7

AND DO YOU KNOW WHY?... DO YOU KNOW WHY I WAS TRYING TO GET YOU BEAT UP?... I'LL TELL YOU WHY!... BECAUSE I AM "MAD-MAN SWEE-BACK"... THE BROCOLLI KING, THAT'S WHY!... I OWN THE BIGGEST BROCOLLI BUSINESS IN THE WORLD, THAT'S WHY!... BUT WHEN KIDS WANT TO GET STRONG DO THEY EAT BROCOLLI?... NO!... BECAUSE OF YOU, THEY CHOOSE SPINACH!
...RIGHT IN THE LABONZA! ...RIGHT IN THE KISHKAS!
BEP
NO! I YAM NOT SMITTY'S BRUDDER HERBY!
...SO WHAT IF THERE'S IRON IN SPINACH! THERE'S IRON IN BROCOLLI!... THERE'S IRON IN PRUNES!... THERE'S IRON IN RAISINS!... BUT WHEN KIDS WANTS TO GET STRONG, THEY CHOOSE GRITTY, LUMPY OLD SPINACH! BECAUSE A MISERABLE, SQUINTY-EYED SAILOR BEATS UP EVERYBODY, THEY CHOOSE SPINACH! THAT'S WHY!
SHOT

SPINACH!
...OY!
...SPINACH!
POOR POOPEYE! THERE'S NO MORE SPINACH LEFT!
HAH! ...AT THE BOTTOM OF THIS GARBAGE PAIL! SOME LEFT OVER SHREDS OF S-S-S-SPINACH!
CHOMP CHOMP GULP!
BROOKLYN DODGERS
INSTANT FRICASEE
POP
I'M POOPEYE THE SAILOR MAN
WHOOM

THAT TAKES CARE OF MAD-MAN SWEE'BACK!... HOW CAN I POSSIBLY EAT BROCOLLI, PRUNES OR RAISINS! DIDN'T THE POOR STUPID FOOL REALIZE THAT I AM BETTER KNOWN AS MAD-MAN POPEYE, THE SPINACH KING?
...THERE'S ONLY ONE THING I CAN'T FIGURE OUT, POOPEYE!.. WHY IS IT THAT YOU DIDN'T GAIN STRENGTH WHEN I GAVE YOU THAT LAST BOWL OF FROZEN SPINACH I HAD IN THE REFRIGERATOR ...HAH?... WHY?... HAH? ...HAH, HAH? WHY?
ELEMENTARY! THAT WAS NO **SPINACH!** THAT WAS **CHARD!**
YOU MEAN IT WAS CHARRED SPINACH?
...NO, IT WAS CHARD!
...SPINACH?
...CHARD!
...CHARRED SPINACH?
...CHARD!
...SPINACH?
...CHARD!
...SPINACH CHARRED?
...NO, CHARD!
SWEE'BACK BURGER---
WINDY'S SIDEWALK CAFE!
8

(Advertisement) (Advertisement)

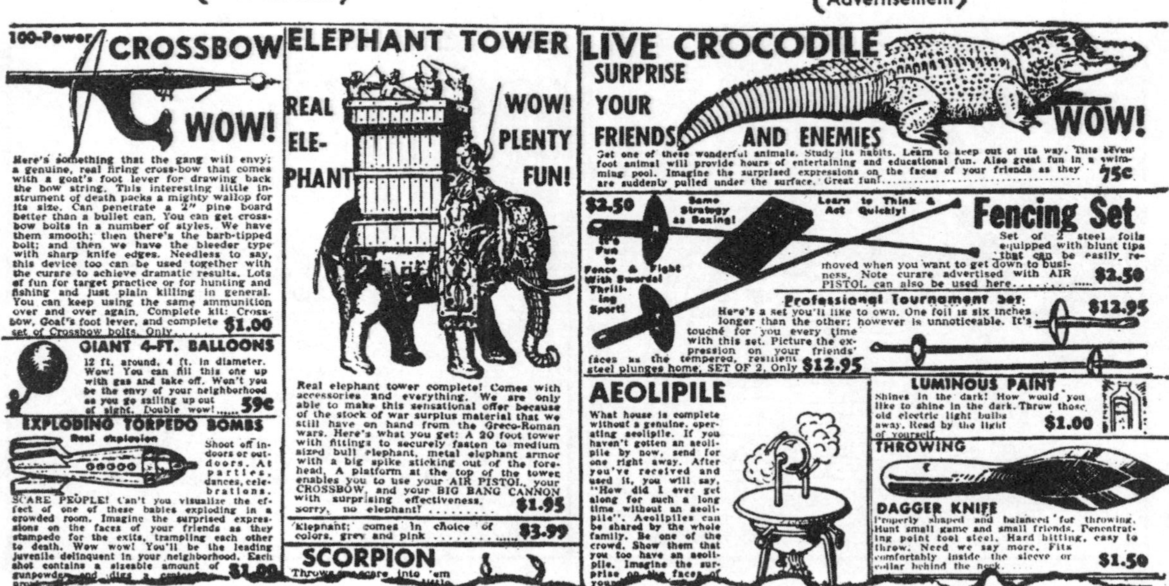

...imately 4 ft. deep...............

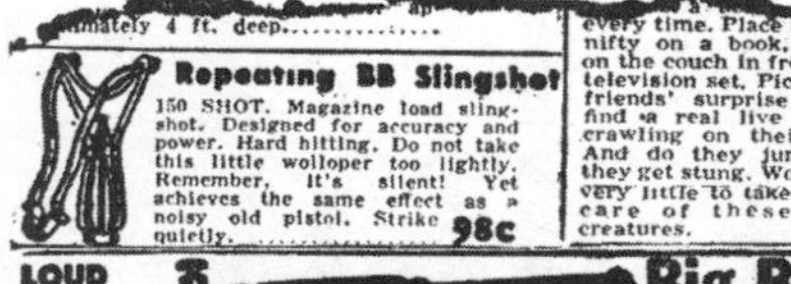

Repeating BB Slingshot

150 SHOT. Magazine load slingshot. Designed for accuracy and power. Hard hitting. Do not take this little wolloper too lightly. Remember, it's silent! Yet achieves the same effect as a noisy old pistol. Strike quietly. **98c**

...every time. Place this little nifty on a book, a table, on the couch in front of the television set. Picture your friends' surprise as they find a real live Scorpion crawling on their collar. And do they jump when they get stung. Wow! Takes very little to take care of these creatures. **$2.50**

...friends when in the middle of nowhere, you whip out your brand-new aeolipile. Wow. The girls will really admire you when they hear that you have an aeolipile. **$14.95**

MUSCLE BUILDER

Build hand, wrist and arm muscles fast. In just a matter of weeks, you'll be able to crush your friends hands to jellied pulp. Picture the expression on your friends' faces. Wow! **Set of 2 with exercise charts...** **$1.25**

STAND OF GRAPE SHOT

Here's a very useful item; a stand of grape shot all ready to load into your Big Bang Cannon. Loaded with 18 solid balls, each 4" in diameter, this baby can do terrible work in a crowd. Won't your friends be surprised as you cut a bloody swath through the gang.......... **$1.98**

LOUD NOISE

• **Realistic**

Big Bang Cannons

Terrific Blast! Brilliant Flash!

Each shot is loud cannon roar with bright flash shooting out of cannon's mouth. Echoes for blocks; real thrill day or night. Used for starting races, noisemaker, celebrations, commanding streets, avenues and approaches; also can be used for knocking down walls, all kinds of demolition purposes. Sounds and looks like a real cannon, only harmless; as long as you don't stand in front of muzzle when firing. Economical to use. (Uses old Civil War army surplus.) Send for price list on solid shot, cannister, grape-shot, etc. Can also be effectively loaded with scrap.

Army olive finish, red wheels.

17-inch Field Gun. With automatic charger —rapid firing. Big, handsome gun. Extremely destructive.................. **$5.50**

28-in. Mammoth Big Bertha Cannon. Tilting body—aim & fire. Terrific shooter. A real Blockbuster................ **$8.50**

Cannon ammunition (not included; order plenty!) can be ordered singly or in carload lots. When ordering please specify amount, whether you just want a single cannon ball or more.

PIKES AND HALBERDS

No home is complete without one of these. You know those uncomfortable situations where his reach is longer than yours and you can't get at him. Well, this is the item you'll want to have. You can do all the damage you want to that bully and he won't get within 7 ft. of you. Notice we are offering pikes and halberds for sticking, hacking, slashing and chopping. Please indicate the type that you want, with your order. Stand 7 ft. away as you watch the surprised expressions on the faces of your friends. Swell for poking fun at people. **$1.50**

2 Passenger Midget Racer Plans **Real Car**

Excellent runabout. Easy to build for about $35. Goes 50 mph; gets 40 m.p. gallon. Uses motorcycle or outboard motor, old auto parts. Fun building. Fun driving. Only hitch is, you have to pedal. Complete Plans. Merely **$2.00**

COMPRESSED AIR TORPEDO WOW!

10 foot copper and gun metal torpedo with war-head, air chamber, engine propellers and rudder. Can attain a speed of 20 miles per hour, and carries enough explosives to wreck any battleship. Sails under water propelled by its own compressed air. Be the first in your neighborhood to get one of these. Can be sailed in the bathtub or in the gutter or any convenient rain-puddle you may find around the house. You can have hours of fun in a swimming-pool or if you are lucky enough to have a battleship floating around somewhere, wow! Of course, this torpedo will work just as well on any ship. If you're at summer camp and you don't like the counsellor, wait till he gets out on the lake in the canoe. They won't even be able to pick him up with a sieve. This torpedo can be obtained in an assortment of colors and war-heads. Please specify whether you want the torpedo with a homing device that tracks the target by itself or whether you want the plain old-fashioned type of torpedo that leaves a horrible white wake behind as it runs at the target. **$1.00**

Thick Lensed Eyeglasses

Heavy duty eyeglasses specially made for readers of our advertisments. You will notice by now, that your eyesight has gone quite bad from reading our small type. Save what's left with these heavy duty glasses. WOW! **$1.98**

10c

SEND 10c for CATALOG of 3000 NOVELTIES

Contains thousands of novelties, tricks, jokes, puzzles, live animals, planes, boats, gadgets, knives, guns, cannons, ammunition, explosives, aardvarks, abaxials, abecedarians, ablatives, abluents, abreactions, abscissas, absorbefacients, acephs, acanthaceouses, acanthocephalans, acanthopterygians, acappellas, acariasises, acarpelouses, acatelectics, acciaccaturas, accipitrines, acelviouses, acephelouses, acerates, acerbates, acervates, acescents, acetanilides, bouncing potrzebies and like that.

"SURE WIN" DICE

WIN ALL! for magic trick or fun. Matched set of fair dice and "sure win" dice. Both pairs look alike, and anyone who wants a pair is a dirty, no-good bum thief **$1.00**

MAIL YOUR ORDERS TO **SMITHSON JOHN & CO., Dept. 98, Wow, Michugan** **ADD 10c ON ALL ORDERS UNDER $1.00**

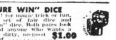

Gonnnnnnnnnnng! The Orient! Our story starts in Hong-Kong . . . center of mystery and intrigue! There, amidst the teeming masses of humanity, ferreting out trouble . . . following suspicious-looking leads with his lovable assistant, Half-Shot Charlie, we find . . .

U HE HEY
EN IS THE
OOT OF ALL
SIN"
HO
UM
NOTA
EPUBLIC
wood.

...WELL, TEDDY AND THE PIRATES! US TROUBLE-SHOOTERS HAVE HAD A PRETTY ROUGH DAY SHOOTING TROUBLE!... SAY... TELL ME... HOW COME YOU CALLED **TEDDY AND THE PIRATES?**
I'LL TELL YOU LATER, HALF-SHOT! RIGHT NOW WE HAVE TO REPORT FOR A NEW ASSIGNMENT!
HONG KONG TONG TU LUNG GONG AND SCHULTZ LTD.
COME IN!
SST, HALF-SHOT! STAND STRAIGHT! THAT'S THE NEW BOSS OF THE TROUBLE-SHOOTING DEPARTMENT! WHY DON'T YOU LIFT YOUR HEAD UP?
IF I DO, MY HAT'LL FALL OFF!
YES, TEDDY AND THE PIRATES...

...I'M THE NEW BOSS! DO YOU RECOGNIZE ME, TEDDY BWAH?
CRIMANETALIES! IT'S PAT...
PAT SLAP
WHAM
WHOMP
KRUMF
IT'S PAT O'BRYAN, HALF-SHOT! PAT AND I ARE OLD BUDDIES, HUH, PAT OL' BUDDY? GOOD OL' PAT!
WHAP
WHOP
WHOMP
...SAILED THE CHINA SEAS FROM RANGOON TO CONEY ISLAND WITH GOOD OL' GREAT OL' PAT... HUH, PAT, HUH? HUH?
THUD!

ENOUGH OF THIS **SNIVELING AFFECTION!** I HAVE HERE YOUR NEXT ASSIGNMENT! AS YOU KNOW, OUR COMPANY RUNS A **GOOD, CLEAN, HONEST** BUSINESS SELLING OPIUM TO THE NATIVES!... SOME DIRTY ROTTEN CROOKS HAVE BEEN HI-JACKING OUR OPIUM SHIPMENTS!
BRATATATATATAT!
FROM THE LOOKS OF THINGS I SUSPECT THAT THE CROOKS, IN ORDER TO GET SHIPPING INFORMATION, HAVE PLACED WITHIN OUR COMPANY AN **INSIDE** MAN! I WANT YOU TWO TO GO **OUTSIDE** AND FIND THIS **INSIDE MAN!** TAKE THAT OPIUM PACKAGE FOR BAIT, AND REMEMBER... **NOTHING MUST STOP YOU FROM CARRYING OUT YOUR ASSIGNMENT!**
DISMISSED!
HEP
HEP
HEP
HEP
HEP
HEP
OPIUM

HMMMM!... FIND AN INSIDE MAN ON THE OUTSIDE! RIDICULOUS!... YOU SEE ANY SUSPICIOUS LEADS, HALF-SHOT?
NOT A THING! ... WAIT! THIS LOOKS LIKE A GOOD LEAD... C'MON!
BAR
NO COVER
NO MINIMUM
ye olde oriental roome
NO FLOOR
TODAY
RIUM
THESE MYSTERIOUS ORIENTAL NIGHT CLUBS USUALLY HAVE GOOD LEADS! GOSH, TEDDY AND THE PIRATES! I WONDER WHO THAT INSIDE MAN IS? I WONDER WHY YOU'RE CALLED TEDDY AND THE PIRATES?
SH... FLOOR SHOW'S BEGINNING! I GOTTA WATCH! IT MIGHT BE A GOOD LEAD!
HEY!
OH THAT ST. LOUIE WOMAN
2

WIT 'ER DIAMOND RINGS
CRIMANETALIES! IT'S BURMA...
HEY!

TEDDY AND THE PIRATES! ... YOU!
IT'S BURMA SHAVE, HALF-SHOT! BURMA AND I ARE OLD BUDDIES, HUH BURMA, OLD BUDDY?
EVERY TIME WE SEE A GOOD LOOK-ING DOLL...
...GOTTA GET READY FOR MY NEXT ACT!
... SAILED THE CHINA SEAS... RANGOON TO CONEY ISLAND... WITH GOOD OL' BURMA... HUH, BURMA? HUH? HUH?
... HE KNOWS 'EM! HE GETS TO HUG 'EM!

...CAN'T TALK TO CUSTOMERS!... BOSS'LL FIRE ME! DON'T CALL ME! ...I'LL CALL YOU!
GOOD OL' BURM'! REMEMBER HOW I HELPED YOU ROLL DRUNKS IN 'FRISCO, BURM'? 'MEMBER, BURM? HUH, BURM?
NAH NYAAHH
MNGRYAAA
SOB BASH!
KICK
AH, MY SWEET! I SEE YOU ARE SPEAKING TO THE CUSTOMERS AGAIN! OH, DEAR! HOW UPSETTING! I SHALL HAVE TO REPRIMAND YOU AGAIN!
EEK! IT'S MY BOSS, SANDTHIRST!... N-NO BOSS! NOT THE BRASS KNUCKLES AGAIN!

TEDDY! STOP HIM! DON'T LET HIM USE THE BRASS KNUCKLES ON ME!
DON'T WORRY, BURM'! I THINK I CAN HANDLE THIS GUY... I THINK! TEDDY AND THE PIRATES ALWAYS HELPS A LADY IN DISTRESS!
SNAP
SNAP
C'MON, HALF-SHOT! YOU PIN HIS ARMS BEHIND HIS BACK WHILE I GIVE HIM A SHOT IN THE HEAD! ...WE ALWAYS HELP A LADY IN DISTRESS...
OOLP!
HEP!
HEP
3

COME, MY DEAR! DO NOT MAKE IT DIFFICULT! FOUR BASHES IS ALL I SHALL GIVE YOU!
TEDDY! EE! TEDDY! EE! OI!
LIKE I SAID... GOTTA TAKE MY SUIT IN FOR A PRESS!... LET'S GO, HALF-SHOT!
HEP
HEP
HEP
HEP
HEP
HEP
HEP
HEP
HEP
HEP
HEP
BESIDES, WE GOT ORDERS, HUH, HALF-SHOT? PAT OBRYAN GAVE US ORDERS...RIGHT, HALF-SHOT? HE TOLD US NOTHING MUST STOP US FROM CARRYING OUT OUR ASSIGNMENT! RIGHT, HALF-SHOT?
RIGHT?
RIGHT?
RIGHT!
RIGHT!
ZOK
POW
SLAM
YOW!
HEP
HEP
HUP!
HEP
HEP
OPIUM

BACK INTO THE TEEMING STREETS OF HONG KONG! YOU FIND MORE TEEMS OUT HERE.. BASEBALL... FOOTBALL TEEMS!...I WONDER IF WE'LL EVER FIND THE INSIDE MAN? I WONDER WHY YOU'RE CALLED 'TEDDY AND THE PIRATES'?
HEY!... GOING INTO THAT DARK DOORWAY...
YALE
DON'T TELL ME YOU SEE ANOTHER OLD BUDDY OF YOURS?
IT'S CONNIE!
CONNIE? ANOTHER BEAUTIFUL GIRL, NO DOUBT! WELL THIS TIME I GET FIRST HUG!
MCMXII

CONNIE, GIRL! I'M TEDDY AND THE PIRATES'S FRIEND, AND ANY FRIEND OF TEDDY AND THE PIRATES IS A FRIEND OF MINE!
WAIT, HALF-SHOT!
C'MERE, GAL!
OPIUM
HONG KONG PING PONG AND MAH JONG CLUB
ZOOOMM
KISS
KISS
KISS
WAIT, HALF-SHOT! ... CONNIE IS...
BOOM
CONNIE IS A MAN!
WHO WAS THAT CRAZY MAN? THAT BOY'S STRICTLY TOM! REAL GONE!
4

IT'S CONNIE... **A-AND BIG-POOP!** MY **OLD** BUDDIES! **SAILED THE CHINA** SEAS... **RANGOON... CONEY** ISLAND... YEAH!
YOU'RE LOOKING REAL, GEORGE, TEDDY AND THE PIRATES!
WHAT'S THAT, BIG-POOP?
OPIUM
GOOD OLD BIG-POOP AN' CONNIE! WE'VE GOTTA TALK OVER OLD TIMES!
BIG-POOP SAYS HE WANTS TO HUG YOUR FRIEND HALF-SHOT... WANTS TO **HUG HIM HELLO!**

...C'MON, CONNIE! LET'S SIT DOWN SOMEWHERE AND TALK OVER OLD TIMES!... C'MON, CONNIE OLD PAL! LEMME BUY YOU A BEER!
BIG-POOP SAYS HE WANTS TO HUG YOU TOO, TEDDY-O'!
SNAP CRACKLE POP
WELL, FLIP MY LID!
AS I WAS SAYING, HALF-SHOT... LET'S GO PACK OUR GEAR!
REMEMBER OUR ASSIGNMENT! WE MUST FIND THE INSIDE MAN AND NOTHING MUST STOP US!
HEP!
HUP!
HEP
HEP
OPIUM

I WONDER WHO THE INSIDE MAN IS? AND FOR THE TENTH TIME... WHY YOU CALLED TEDDY AND THE PIRATES!
SH, HALF-SHOT! WE'RE NEAR-ING THE WATER-FRONT!
CRIMANETALIES! LOOK SEE, THAT OLD CHINESE JUNK TIED UP BY THE WATERFRONT?
YEAH?
YEH? YEH?
THE CAPTAIN OF THIS JUNK IS THE ROUGHEST, MEANEST, NASTIEST, TOUGHEST CAPTAIN ON THE HIGH SEAS, AND I KNOW THE CAPTAIN!
... AN OLD BUDDY OF YOURS, I'LL BET! WELL, YOU GO HUG YOUR BUDDIES ALONE, THIS TIME! I'M FINISHED!
OPIUM

BY GEORGE! THIS CAPTAIN IS THE DRAGGING LADY! MY OLD BUDDY!
...SAILED THE CHINA SEAS TOGETHER! HIYA, DRAG!
AH! IT IS THE YELLOW-HAIRED ONE! APPROACH THE DRAGGING LADY, YELLOW-HAIRED ONE!
HEY, HALF-SHOT! YOU SURE YOU DON'T WANT TO MEET MY GOOD OL' BUDDY, DRAGGING LADY?
BAM
BASH
HIT!
HIT!
BOUND!

GOSH, TEDDY AND THE PIRATES! SHE'S REAL PEACHY KEEN **WOW! ROWF ROWF!**
INTRODUCE ME, HUH? WILLYA, TEDDY? WILLYA? WILLYA?
WHEE!
WOO WOO!
DRIP
...AND, YELLOW-HAIRED ONE, WHO IS THIS BANG-HAIRED ONE WHO YAMMERS LIKE A MONKEY?
MONKEY, HUH? I KNOW THIS DAME'S TYPE, TEDDY! THEY ACT TOUGH AND BUSINESS-LIKE ON THE OUTSIDE, BUT UNDERNEATH IT ALL, THEY'RE **FEMININE... CRINGING... DELICATE...** LIKE ANY OTHER WOMAN... **TREAT 'EM ROUGH,** I SAY!
COME'RE, YOU DRAGGING LADY!
EXCUSE ME A MOMENT, BANG-HAIRED ONE!

ALL RIGHT, YOU SWINE! WE'RE CASTING OFF! YOU, RED-HAIRED ONE... HOIST THE MAIN-SAIL! SNAP TO!
YES, MASTER!
SWISH
KNAP

STEP LIVELY, YOU BABOONS! LOWER THE JIB! BATTEN THE HATCHES! YOU, BALD-HEADED ONE! YOU'RE MOVING TOO SLOWLY!
KNOP
YES, MASTER!
HARD-A-LEE ON THE STARBOARD BOW!
YOU... TWO-HEADED ONE... YOU STUMBLED AGAINST ME! SHVIENHUNT!
YES, MASTER!
POW
POW
POW
6

THERE!... THAT GOT THIS JUNK GOING!
NOW... BANG-HAIRED ONE! WHAT WAS IT YOU WERE SAYING ABOUT **MY TYPE OF WOMAN?**
ME SAY SOMETHIN'? I DIDN'T SAY NOTHIN'! YOU HEAR ME SAY SOMETHIN', TEDDY? TEDDY SAID SOMETHIN'! NOT **ME!**
NOW, YELLOW-HAIRED ONE! TELL ME ABOUT DARK-HAIRED ONE... PAT O'BRYAN!
...WHY DO YOU INTERRUPT, POINTY-HEADED ONE?
MASTER! MASTER! HELP! HELP! A STRANGE CRAFT IS BEARING DOWN UPON US!

I KNOW WHAT THAT CRAFT IS! IT IS A BAND OF HI-JACKERS!
HERE, YELLOW-HAIRED ONE AND BANG-HAIRED ONE! TAKE THESE CUTLASSES!
WE'LL PROTECT YOU, DRAGGING LADY!
ALL HANDS AND FEET ON DECK! STAND BY TO REPEL BOARDERS! WE WILL FIGHT THEM ON THE LAND... IN THE AIR!
RIGHT, DRAGGING LADY!
WATCH OUT FOR THAT ONE, DRAGGING LADY!
CRASH
KLASH
SLASH
BASH
GASH

...WE WILL FIGHT THEM ON THE BEACHES TILL WE ARE COM-PLETELY EXHAUSTED! ALLA TIME WE WILL FIGHT, FIGHT, FIGHT!
RIGHT, DRAGGING LADY!
GET THAT ONE, DRAGGING LADY!

WE WILL FIGHT THEM TILL EVERY LAST DROP OF OUR BLOOD IS SPILT! ...TILL WE ARE COMPLETELY DEAD AND HACKED TO LITTLE PIECES!
HEP HEP HEP HEP
OPIUM
WRONG, DRAGGING LADY!
HEP HEP HEP HEP
REMEMBER THE WORDS OF OUR IMMORTAL PAT O'BRYAN!... NOTHING MUST STOP US FROM CARRYING OUT OUR ASSIGNMENT...
HEP HEP HEP HEP HEP
OPIUM
...OUR ASSIGNMENT TO FIND THE INSIDE MAN!
HEP HEP HEP
'BYE!

WELL, HERE WE ARE, ABOUT TO WALK THE PLANK OFF OF THE HIJACKERS' SHIP! BUT BEFORE I GO, THERE IS SOMETHING I MUST KNOW... SOMETHING I'VE GOT TO KNOW BEFORE MY SOUL IS EVER TO REST IN PEACE!

I'VE GOT TO KNOW THE ANSWER TO TWO QUESTIONS... FIRST... WHO IS THE INSIDE MAN WE'RE LOOKING FOR, AND SECOND... WHY DO THEY CALL YOU 'TEDDY AND THE PIRATES'?

HUP..
HOO BOY
TOINGG
SUDDENLY... IT ALL COMES CLEAR TO ME...
...I NOW KNOW WHO THE INSIDE MAN FOR THE OPIUM HIJACKERS IS...
...AND I KNOW WHY THEY CALL HIM 'TEDDY AND THE PIRATES'!...

YUMMY!
SWISH
LUNCH!
GET 'IM!
GNASH
GOBBLE
CHOMP
GULP
SMACK
SNAP CRACKLE POP
CRIMANETALIES, HALF-SHOT...
AND I WANTED YOU TO MEET SOME MORE BUDDIES THAT SAILED THE CHINA SEAS WITH ME!...I WANTED YOU TO MEET '*THE PIRATES*'!
OPIUM
8

THEN HERE'S THAT FEATURE YOU ALL KNOW AND LOVE.. BUT IF YOU THINK IT'S INTERESTING NOW..YOU SHOULD'VE SEEN IT IN THE OLD DAYS! YOU OLD-TIMERS KNOW WHAT WE MEAN!.. REMEMBER WHEN THEY FIRST STARTED PRINTING IT? 'MEMBER, YOU OLD-TIMERS?.. IT WAS REAL QUEER..REAL WEIRD..REAL ECHHHH!...YOU KNOW..LIKE PEOPLE WHO READ MAD!...'MEMBER YOU BUSTED-DOWN OLD-TIMERS YOU?...OF COURSE, WE'RE TALKING ABOUT
RIPUP'S
Believe It or Don't!

THE HUMAN PINCUSHION
GUNG GOHOME, Hindu Ascetic, WALKED IN THE HOT SUN with 50 sharp spear-like pins embedded in his flesh – to make pennance – to punish self – but mainly to help wife who was sewing new veil and needed pin-cushion!

SYMBOL OF DEATH!
SACRED SOUTH AMERICAN INDIAN SYMBOL, WHEN GAZED UPON, CAUSES DEATH WITHIN THE YEAR!
Too bad if You looked
MELVIN FURD of Banff, Vt., is a MARTIAN!

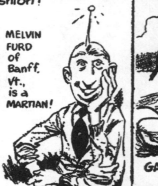

THE TALLEST MAN IN THE WORLD–
GALUSHA STURDLEY of Poomtang, O. is the tallest man in the world. Note size of hand.
(figure on left is not Galusha but his father, Zane Sturdley)
GALUSHA IS HAND FATHER ZANE IS STANDING UPON!
Rrrrrrrrrip.

...'MEMBER? HAH?... 'MEMBER THE WAY HE'D SHOW A GUY WHO COULD STICK HIS ELBOW IN HIS EAR?... OR THE GUY WHO HANGS BY HIS EYEBALLS?... OR THE GUY WHO COULD STICK HIS ELBOW IN HIS EYEBALLS WHILE HANGING BY HIS EAR? BUT MAINLY HE'D DIG UP THESE UNBELIEVABLE FACTS YOU'D NEVER BELIEVE IN A MILLION YEARS... FULLY AUTHENTICATED, FULLY DOCUMENTED, AND APPROVED BY PARENTS MAGAZINE... LIKE FORINSTANCE...

RIPUP'S — Believe It or Don't!

JOSEPH STALIN

WAS BORN IN THE BRONX!

HE WORKED HIS WAY THROUGH COLLEGE
SELLING MAGAZINE SUBSCRIPTIONS,
AND THEN WENT WEST TO BE A COWBOY
BEFORE HE CROSSED THE OCEAN
AND BECAME DICTATOR OF
RUSSIA!

NIAGARA FALLS DOES ***NOT*** FALL!

It actually rises-but in such a way as to create an illusion of falling. For years, Honeymooners have believed that Niagara Falls is falling!
THE EARTH HAS 10 YEARS TO LIVE!
A comet is heading DIRECTLY TOWARDS EARTH and is due to smash it into oblivion in APRIL, 1955!
5+3-2=7248
FIRE IS A LIQUID!
Rrrrrrrip

...'MEMBER?... BUT THAT WAS YEARS AGO, AS YOU OLD-TIMERS... YOU BUSTED-DOWN RACKETTY OLD-TIMERS... REMEMBER! MEANWHILE, RIPUP IS FOR MANY YEARS, GONE FROM THE SCENE! NEVERTHELESS, "BELIEVE IT OR DON'T" CONTINUES... BUT SOMEHOW, IT'S NOT THE SAME!... SOMEHOW... SOMEWHERE... SOMETIME... SOMEHOW... SOMEWHERE... IT IS DIFFERENT!.. THE EUCHHH IS GONE!... YOU SEE... EUCHHH HAS BEEN REPLACED BY YECHHH!... LIKE FORINSTANCE...
RIPUP'S — Believe It or Don't!
RENFREW ZETS FELL FROM A 50 STORY WINDOW-
AND LIVED!

Fortunately, there was a fire escape outside the window.

HE ALWAYS READS SIDEWAYS!

Eddie Ptung reads his Chinese language newspaper up to down instead of left to right!

SERUTAN
spelled backwards is
NATURES

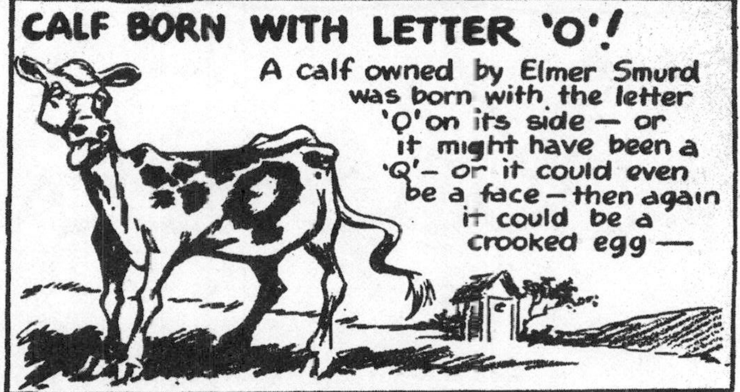

CALF BORN WITH LETTER 'O'!

A calf owned by Elmer Smurd was born with the letter 'O' on its side — or it might have been a 'Q'— or it could even be a face — then again it could be a crooked egg —

OPTICAL ILLUSION

Sent in by Robert Hall

JACKET SEEMS TO TURN INSIDE-OUT, YET STAYS OUTSIDE-IN AND VISA-VERSA! (And why not? It's a reversible!)

Comparison Dept.: Did you ever read any authentic stuff on the old Wild West? . . . I mean real authentic! . . . Next, did you ever compare it with the movie and television version of the old Wild West? Ain't it a howl? . . . For instance, to be specific, take the . . .

FIRST OF ALL, IN MOVIES AND TELEVISION, THE COWBOY IS USUALLY NAMED SOME-THING LIKE... ***LANCE STERLING!***... NOT THAT YOU'D MEET ONE GUY IN A HUNDRED WITH SUCH A NAME!...

NOW IN REAL LIFE... THE 100% GENUINE COWBOY HAD AN ORDINARY OLD NAME LIKE MAYBE... ***JOHN SMURD!***... THEY'D HANG ANYBODY WITH A NAME LIKE LANCE STERLING!

MAINLY PEOPLE HAVE NAMES LIKE...GEORGE FREEBLE ..IGGY SIEDENHAM...MELVIN POZNOWSKI...!COULD YOU EVER PICTURE A COWBOY HERO CALLED MELVIN POZNOWSKI?...SO HIS NAME IS LANCE STERLING!AND HIS CLOTHES...OH BROTHER!...HAND TAILORED!...WITH GLOVES!...IN THE HOT SUN ALL DAY LONG, WITH GLOVES! ..ANYBODY HERE EVER WEAR GLOVES IN THE HOT SUN ALL DAY LONG?... YOU BETCHA YOU DIDN'T! YOU'D GET A RASH AND YOUR HANDS WOULD ROT OFF!

AND IF THEY COULD GROW THEM MOST GENUINE COWBOYS HAD BIG WALRUS MUSTACHES WHICH WERE THE CUSTOM OF THE TIMES! CAN YOU IMAGINE ANYTHING MORE NAUSEATING THAN THE HOLLYWOOD COWBOY WITH SUCH A NAUSEATING MUSTACHE, GOING INTO A CLINCH WITH THE LEADING LADY?... NAUSEATING MAINLY SINCE THESE MUSTACHES OFTEN HAD TOBACCO JUICE SOAKED IN! AS FOR CLOTHES... LET'S FACE IT! WHAT DO YOU HAVE TO WEAR TO TEND COWS BESIDE A GOOD PAIR OF BOOTS?

IN MOVIES... LANCE STERLING NEVER WORKS! ...HE RUNS FROM POSSES!... HE HAS FIST FIGHTS! ...HE SHOOTS IT OUT WITH THE BAD GUYS!... BUT HE NEVER WORKS! NOW TELL ME HOW CAN A GUY SUPPORT HIMSELF IF HE NEVER WORKS?
AUCTION

OLD JOHN SMURD WORKED LIKE A HORSE! HIS HORSE WORKED LIKE OLD JOHN SMURD! THERE WASN'T NO COWBOY UNION THEN! WHO HAD TIME FOR RUNNING FROM POSSES? WHO HAD TIME FOR SHOOTING IT OUT WITH BAD GUYS?

$50.00
REWARD
DEAD

LANCE STERLING ALWAYS HAS PLENTY TIME FOR TROUBLE ... AND IS USUALLY SOME NO-GOOD-NICK HANGING AROUND WITH A THIN BLACK MUSTACHE AND A BLACK HAT! EVERY TIME... A THIN BLACK MUSTACHE AND A BLACK HAT...
$5,000.00 REWARD ALIVE
Flip
AS FOR VILLIANS IN JOHN SMURD'S TIME... ONLY A GIGOLO FURRINER'D WEAR A THIN BLACK MUSTACHE! VILLIAN'S MUSTACHE IN JOHN SMURD'S TIME (EXCEPT MAYBE FOR SMELL) WAS JUST LIKE JOHN SMURD'S MUSTACHE!
$50.00 REW DEAD!
WILLY THE KIDDY
REWARD

NOW IN THE MOVIES WHEN THE HERO PULLS HIS GUN, HERE'S WHERE THE REAL PHONEY BALONEY BEGINS!
K-KLIK

OLD LANCE STERLING, SIMPLE COWPOKE, WHIPS OUT HIS GUN LIKE THE CIRCUS TRICK SHOOTER!

JOHN SMURD DIDN'T HAVE MUCH EQUIPMENT AND HAD TO DRAG ***HIS*** SHOOTING IRON OUT OF HIS SHIRT OR PANTS POCKET!
PTEEE

...MAIN THING WAS TO HAVE RIGID ARM...STEADY EYE...OR IN OTHER WORDS, MAIN THING WAS NOT TO BE SCAIRT.
PTEEEEE
RIP
2

THE WAY LANCE FANS OFF SIX SHOTS IN ¼ OF A SECOND... HE'D HAVE TO PRACTICE FIVE HOURS A DAY!
Blam Six Times
NOW I DON'T CARE IF YOU'RE ANNIE OAKLEY! YOU GOT TO MISS YOUR TARGET SOME-TIMES!...NOT OLD LANCE!

MEANWHILE ALL THIS TIME OLD JOHN'D STILL BE AIMING... NOT ANY OF THAT FROM THE HIP STUFF, EITHER!
ZOOO
BDEEEE

...AND HE'D OF BLOW'D THE VILLIAN'S HEAD OFF IF... AS OFTEN HAPPENS IN REAL LIFE... HIS GUN DIDN'T JAM!
CLUNK
BDOOO

NOW GET THIS!... HERE'S THIS VILLIAN WHO'S JUST TRIED TO MURDER LANCE... JUST TRIED TO **MURDER** HIM... I ASK YOU... WHAT DOES LANCE DO?... OLD LANCE **THROWS HIS GUN AWAY AND GOES TO FIGHT THE VILLIAN FAIR FIST-FIGHT STYLE!**

JOHN SMURD... HIS VILLIAN, MIGHT'VE BEEN NERVOUS AND MISSED HIM WITH ALL SIX SHOTS! OLD JOHN MIGHT'VE THROWN HIS GUN AWAY TOO... ONLY THE REASON HE'D THROWN IT WAS BECAUSE HE WAS TRYING TO BUST THE VILLIAN'S HEAD OPEN!

NOW COMES THE FIST-FIGHT! HERE THIS GUY HAS JUST TRIED TO MURDER HIM... LANCE STER-LING COMES OUT FIGHTING WITH ONLY FISTS ALLOWED! NATURALLY, VILLIAN BUSTS HIM ON THE HEAD WITH A NEARBY ARMCHAIR!
CRASH!
NOW IF JOHN SMURD GOT HIT WITH AN ARMCHAIR ... YOU THINK THAT CHAIR WOULD FLY TO FLIN-DERS LIKE THEM HOLLYWOOD BALSA-WOOD CHAIRS? THAT CHAIR WOULDN'T FLY TO FLINDERS! MORE THAN LIKELY, JOHN SMURD'D FLY TO FLINDERS!
CRUNK!
3

BACK TO LANCE STER-LING!...THERE HE IS ... HELPLESS... WITH THE VILLIAN ABOUT TO TROMP HIM!

...HE COULD COME TO IN A SECOND... A MINUTE...AN HOUR...BUT ***NO!*** HE COMES TO ***JUST*** AS THE BOOT COMES DOWN!
TROMP
OLD JOHN... HE'D'VE LAID THERE TOO! ONLY DIFFERENCE WAS...WHEN THAT CHAIR'D'VE HIT HIM...MAN, HE'D BE ***OUT!***

...DON'T MATTER IF THE VILLIAN TRIED TO KICK HIM IN THE FACE OR NOT... HE'D'VE BEEN ***OH-YOU-TEE... OUT!***
TROMP

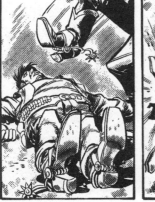

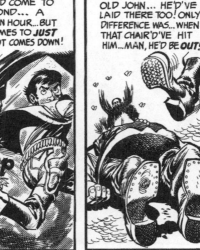

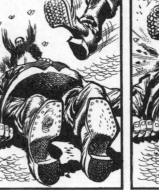

...OLD LANCE, HE'S UP THERE STILL FIGHTING FAIR... AND HE GIVES THE VILLIAN A BIG KNOCK IN THE HEAD!
WOK
...AND THE VILLIAN GIVES HIM A KNOCK IN THE HEAD! WHICH...IF YOU WENT BY THE SOUND EFFECT ...WOULD KILL AN ELEPHANT!
WOK
JOHN SMURD...HE'D'VE STILL BEEN OUT! I MEAN OH-YOU-TEE! BUT YOU COULDN'T FEEL TOO MAD AT THE VILLIAN...
TROMP TROMP
...BECAUSE IF JOHN'D REACHED THE CHAIR FIRST, HE'D'VE BEEN TROMPING THE VILLIAN! ...MAN!...OH-YOU-TEE!
TROMP TROMP TROMP

HALF AN HOUR LATER, THIS BIG MOVIE FIGHT ENDS WHERE LANCE, TO WIND IT UP, GIVES THIS VILLIAN SUCH A SMECK... THE VILLIAN GOES CRASHING OVER THE COUNTER, CRASHING THROUGH A PILE OF BARRELS THAT COME CRASHING DOWN...
BOOM!

MEANWHILE, JOHN SMURD... HE'D'VE STILL BEEN OH-YOU-TEE... **OUT!** IF **YOU** EVER GOT HIT ON THE HEAD WITH A GOOD STOUT OLD CHAIR WITH A HAND CARVED SEAT-BOARD AND PEGGED JOINTS, YOU'D KNOW WHAT I MEAN!
TROMPITTY
TROMP
TROMP
TROMP
TROMP
4

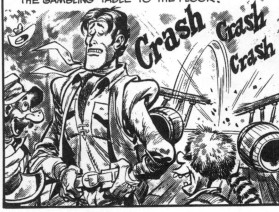

BACK AT THAT MOVIE FIGHT AFTER CRASHING THROUGH THE BARRELS, THE VILLIAN KEEPS CRASHING BACK THROUGH THE DOOR THROUGH THE RAILING WHERE HE CRASHES DOWN ON THE GAMBLING TABLE TO THE FLOOR!

Crash Crash Crash

ON THE OTHER HAND, THE END OF JOHN SMURD'S FIGHT WOULD'VED ENDED WITH OLD JOHN STILL OH-YOU-TEE AND A MONTH LATER, OLD JOHN WOULD'VE SNUCK UP ON THE VIL-LIAN AND BLOW'D HIS HEAD OFF!
BOOM

AND SO, THE CITIZENS THANK LANCE STERLING FOR AGAIN BRINGING LAW AND ORDER TO ANOTHER TOWN!

...AND IF THEY'D HAD GIRLS LIKE THIS, THE WILD WEST WOULD'VE BEEN A LOT WILDER!

THE CITIZENS MIGHT'VE TURNED OUT FOR OLD COWBOY JOHN SMURD TOO (BEING CAREFUL TO STAY UPWIND)...

...AND IF YOU'RE INTERESTED... THIS IS WHAT THE GIRL HE'D HANG AROUND WITH, MIGHT'VE LOOKED LIKE!

AS THE SUN SETS ON LANCE STERLING, HE LEAVES THE PARTY-MAKING AND THE DANCING AND RIDES AWAY WITH THE GIRL...PLAYING GUITAR WITH A PHILOHARMONIC ORCHESTRA ACCOMPANIMENT IN THE BACKGROUND!
AND YOU CAN BET WHEREVER THIS COWPUNCHER GOES ...THERE'LL BE MORE COWPUNCHERS PUNCHED THAN COWS!

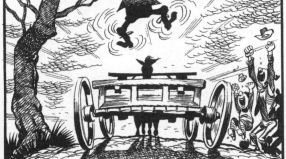

AND AS THE SUN SET ON THE REAL AUTHENTIC WILD WEST... JOHN SMURD TOO MIGHT'VE LEFT THE PARTY-MAKING AND THE DANCING!... ONLY DIFFERENCE IS IT'D PROBABLY BE A NECKTIE PARTY AND HE'D'VE BEEN THE ONLY ONE DANCING!

WHAT WITH PLENTY OTHER PROBLEMS, WHO NEEDED BUMS AROUND WHO WERE ALWAYS GETTING IN TROUBLE!

5

PUZZLE PAGE!

HIDDEN ANIMALS

ANOTHER PAGE CHOCK FULL O' PUZZLE FUN! IN THE FIRST PICTURE, OUR CLEVER ARTIST HAS CLEVERLY CONCEALED ANIMALS... CRAFTILY BLENDING THEM IN WITH THE GROUND, THE TREES, AND THE SKY! CAN YOU FIND THEM?

NEXT, IN THE SECOND PICTURE, OUR FOXY OLD ARTIST HAS HIDDEN 115 ANIMALS! CAN YOU FIND THEM?

NEXT, OUR ARTIST, (CLEVER RASCAL) HAS HIDDEN HIMSELF 'CAUSE WE NEED HIS DRAWINGS FOR THE NEXT ISSUE AND IT'S PAST THE DEADLINE!... CAN YOU FIND HIM?

ANSWERS ON LAST PAGE!

With this story . . . we, the writers of MAD, are coming closer to something more horrifying, more frightening than anything before . . . and that thing is (shudder). . . that thing is (gagg) . . . is . . . IS. . . . The day we're going to run out of material! . . . Oh, well . . . on with our story . . . called . . .

MANDUCK THE MAGICIAN

HOOHAH... MANDUCK IN TROUBLE... AND ME, LOATHAR, HIS TRUSTY ASSISTANT, CANNOT HELP 'CAUSE HIM IN GRIP OF BIG MONSTER OCTOPUS WRAPPED ALL AROUND HIM TIGHT! ME WONDER HOW MANDUCK GET OUT OF DIS? ME WONDER IF HIM GESTURE HYPNO-TICALLY? ME WONDER IF HIM TURN OCTOPUS INTO SOMETHING? ME WONDER WHAT HIM TURN OCTOPUS INTO?
...MANDUCK GESTURES HYPNOTICALLY...
POFF!
CRUNK!
CRAK!
BILL ELDER

HO! DAT MANDUCK! HIM IS ALWAYS HAVIN' SUCH GLAMOROUS, EXCITING LIFE! HIM ALWAYS HAVIN' ADVENTURES... ALWAYS IN TROUBLE! **HO!... DERE MANDUCK NOW!**
EEEEEEEK!
HEY, MANDUCK! WHERE YOU GOIN'?... YOU GOIN' ON EXCITING ADVENTURES?... YOU GOIN' TO FAR OFF GLAMOROUS PLACES?
DINING CAR TO THE REAR
7
6
...YOU GOIN' ON SOME SCIENCE-FICTION TYPE ADVENTURE?... YOU GOIN' ON SOME WEIRD FANTASY TYPE ADVENTURE?... HUH, MANDUCK?... HUH?... HUH?
HUH?
HUH?
THIS IS CINERAMA

WHERE AM I GOING? WHERE AM I GOING?
...WHERE DO YOU THINK I'M GOING!
...I'M GOING TO WORK... AS USUAL!
...ANOTHER DAY...ANOTHER DOLLAR!
DAT RIGHT! DIS IS WEEKDAY!... YOU ONLY GOT TIME FOR GLAMOROUS ADVENTURES ON SATURDAY AND SUNDAY! YOU GOTTA WORK ON WEEKDAYS!...HEY! WHY YOU RUNNIN'? YOU CONSCIENTIOUS 'BOUT GETTING TO WORK ON TIME? YOU GOTTA PUNCH TIME CLOCK?
RELAY TEAM 3
WHY AM I RUNNING? WHY AM I RUNNING?
...WHY DO YOU THINK I'M RUNNING!
...I'M RUNNING FROM THE LAW AS USUAL!
...ANOTHER DAY, ANOTHER COPPER!

IT'S GETTING SO'S A HARD WORKING PITCHMAN CAN'T SET UP A SELLING TABLE ON A STREET CORNER ANYMORE WITHOUT BEING CHASED BY A POLICEMAN!
WAIT!... I GOT A GOOD IDEA HOW TO GET AWAY FROM HIM!... I ONCE SAW THIS TRICK DONE IN THE MOVIES!
This is your Life Errol Flynn
This is your Life King Farouk
QUICK, LADY, QUICK, QUICK! MAKE BELIEVE WE'RE LOVERS! QUICK! OOH! OOH! I CAN'T EXPLAIN! QUICK! QUICK! MAKE BELIEVE!

I DON'T UNDERSTAND IT! THAT TRICK WORKED WHEN I ONCE SAW IT DONE IN THE MOVIES!
I GOT ONE MORE TRICK LEFT, AND IF THAT DON'T WORK... WHO KNOWS... I **MAY** HAVE TO GESTURE HYPNOTICALLY!
ZOO
(PUFF)! WE GOTTUM AWAY (PUFF)! DAT MUS' BE SOME TRICK YOU USED (PUFF)! TO GET AWAY (PUFF)! HOW YOU DO DAT DERE DAT?
WELL... DID YOU NOTICE THAT GIRL'S SLIP WAS SHOWING?
...YES! ...YES YES! ...YES! ...YES!
DID YOU NOTICE HOW THE POLICEMAN WAS ABOUT TO GRAB ME?
...YES YES YES! ...YES YES! ...YES!
WELL, I GAVE HIM THE **SLIP!**
This is Your Life Lassie
SMEK
2

O.K., LOATHAR! THIS STORY'S MOVING PRETTY SLOW SO LET'S GO TO WORK! THIS LOOKS LIKE A GOOD CORNER TO SET UP OUR STAND!
GASOLINE ALLEY
...PUT UP MY SIGN, FOR THE SIGN OF MANDUCK THE MAGICIAN IS KNOWN THROUGH-OUT THE LAND AND WHEN PEOPLE SEE MY SIGN, THEY GATHER AROUND WHEN THEY SEE MY FAMOUS SIGN!
YESSIR! PEOPLE LOVE THE SIGHT OF THAT SIGN!... NEVER GET TIRED OF IT MYSELF!
PICK A CARD!
GEE, WURLITZER- IT'S A DAD!

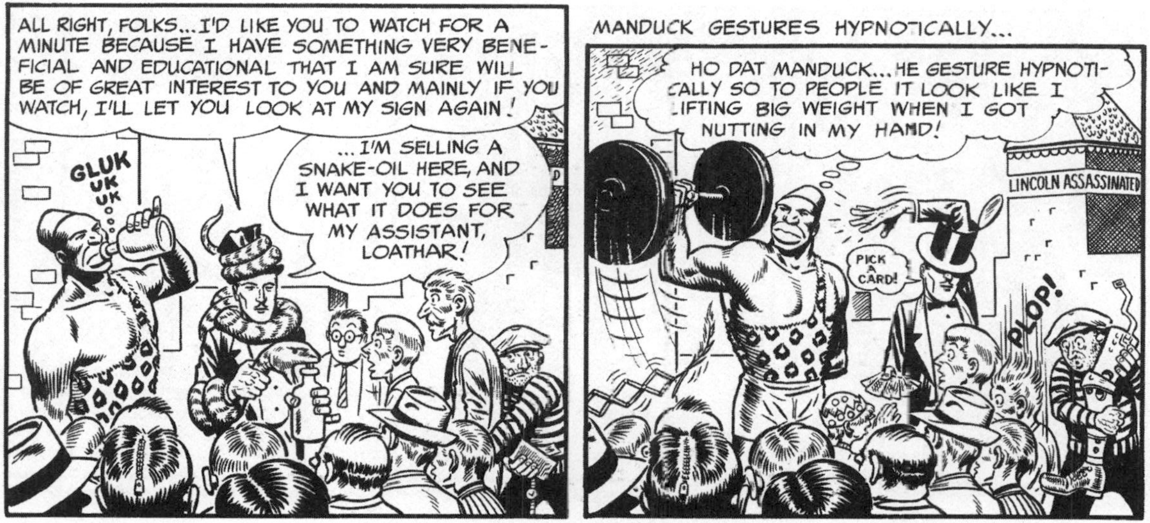

ALL RIGHT, FOLKS...I'D LIKE YOU TO WATCH FOR A MINUTE BECAUSE I HAVE SOMETHING VERY BENEFICIAL AND EDUCATIONAL THAT I AM SURE WILL BE OF GREAT INTEREST TO YOU AND MAINLY IF YOU WATCH, I'LL LET YOU LOOK AT MY SIGN AGAIN!

GLUK UK UK

...I'M SELLING A SNAKE-OIL HERE, AND I WANT YOU TO SEE WHAT IT DOES FOR MY ASSISTANT, LOATHAR!

MANDUCK GESTURES HYPNOTICALLY...

HO DAT MANDUCK...HE GESTURE HYPNOTICALLY SO TO PEOPLE IT LOOK LIKE I LIFTING BIG WEIGHT WHEN I GOT NUTTING IN MY HAND!

LINCOLN ASSASSINATED

PICK A CARD!

PLOP!

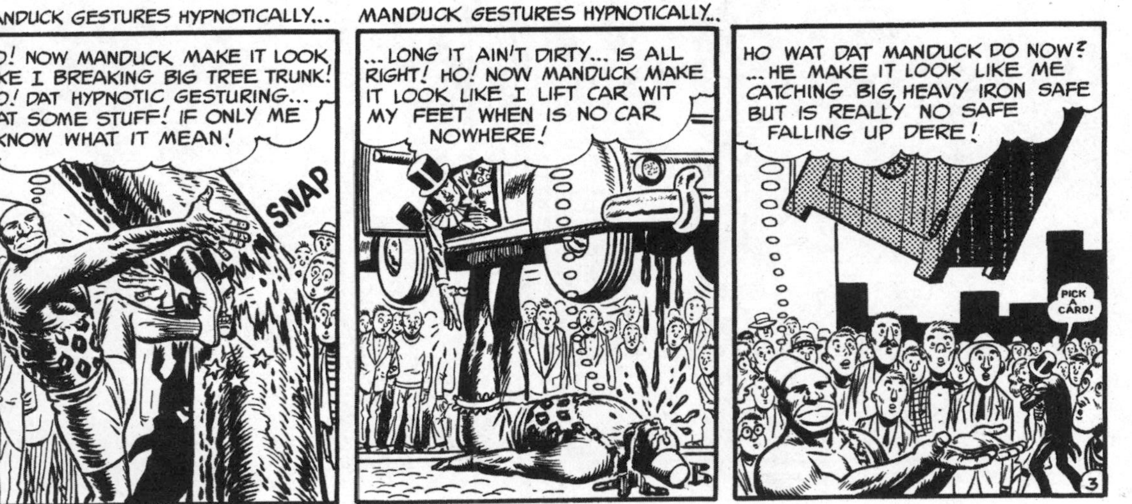
MANDUCK GESTURES HYPNOTICALLY...
HO! NOW MANDUCK MAKE IT LOOK LIKE I BREAKING BIG TREE TRUNK! HO! DAT HYPNOTIC GESTURING... DAT SOME STUFF! IF ONLY ME KNOW WHAT IT MEAN!
SNAP
MANDUCK GESTURES HYPNOTICALLY...
...LONG IT AIN'T DIRTY... IS ALL RIGHT! HO! NOW MANDUCK MAKE IT LOOK LIKE I LIFT CAR WIT MY FEET WHEN IS NO CAR NOWHERE!
HO WAT DAT MANDUCK DO NOW? ...HE MAKE IT LOOK LIKE ME CATCHING BIG, HEAVY IRON SAFE BUT IS REALLY NO SAFE FALLING UP DERE!
PICK A CARD!
3

HEY! MANDUCK! WAT YOU DO? WHY I FEEL SO FUNNY WHEN I CATCH DAT SAFE DAT YOU MAKE IT LOOK LIKE IS FALLING ON ME WHEN YOU GESTURE HYPNOTICALLY?
...SAFE? WHAT SAFE?... I DIDN'T MAKE NO HYPNOTIC GESTURE FOR NO SAFE... DIDN'T MAKE NO HYPNOTIC GESTURE IN THE LAST 5 MINUTES!
BING CROSBY ENTER-PRIZES.
IODINE
ALL RIGHT, FOLKS! YOU'VE SEEN WHAT MY SNAKE OIL DID FOR LOATHAR!... IT CAN DO IT FOR YOU! ...HURRY AND BUY YOUR BOTTLE NOW!... I'VE ONLY GOT A FEW LEFT... ONLY FORTY-SEVEN THOUSAND AND TWELVE BOTTLES LEFT!
YOU WANT ONE SIR?
...WATCH WHAT HAP-PENS WHEN HE DRINKS MY SNAKE-OIL!
STRIKE IT RICH INC.

MANDUCK GESTURES HYPNOTICALLY...
NOT BAD!
NOT BAD AT ALL!
'COURSE IT'S NOT BAD- IT'S MISERABLE!!
GOSH, MANDUCK... YOU'VE GIVEN ME A NEW BODY! THERE'S A BULLY AT THE BEACH WHO'S ALWAYS BEEN KICKING SAND IN MY EYES AND CALLING ME 'SKINNY'!... NOW I'LL SHOW HIM!
DIAL 'M' FOR MONEY LEAVANARM LOAN WOLF CO.
I WAS RAISED ON CHICKEN FAT.
ALL RIGHT, FOLKS! $1.00 A BOTTLE! DON'T RUSH! THERE'S PLENTY FOR EVERYONE! QUIT RUSHING! STOP RUSHING! DO NOT RUSH... BECAUSE MAINLY YOU'RE RUSHING IN THE WRONG DIRECTION!
DOESN'T ANYONE WANT THIS SNAKE-OIL I'M SELLING?
DO YOU WANT THIS SNAKE-OIL I'M SELLING?
ISN'T YOUR FACE FAMI-LIAR?
WHY STAY RUPTURED!

LIKE I SAID... DOESN'T ANYONE WANT SNAKE-OIL I'M SMELLING! I'M SMELLING SNAKE-OIL! SMELLING... NOT SELLING!
WAIT A MINUTE, LOATHAR! THIS SITUATION REMINDS ME OF A TRICK I ONCE SAW IN THE MOVIES...
TELEPHONE DIRECTORY
MANISCHEWITZ
HEY! YOU TRY DAT TRICK ONE TIME AN' IT DON'T WORK!... YOU TRY DAT TRICK SECOND TIME AN' IT DON'T WORK! WHY ALLA TIME YOU TRY DAT TRICK IF IT DON'T WORK?
WHO CARES IF IT DON'T WORK?
LADIES SHOWER ROOM
4

HEY, MANDUCK! CUT OUT BALONEY AND T'ROW DAT POLICEMAN COUPLA HYPNOTIC GESTURES!
WELL...I HATE TO UNLEASH MY HYPNOTIC POWERS AGAINST THE LAW! WHEN ONE HAS MY HYPNOTIC GESTURE, ONE MUST USE IT WISELY... MORALLY... FOR THE GOOD OF MANKIND...
...BY GEORGE... HE IS GETTING CLOSE...
MICKEY SPILLANE
MANDUCK GESTURES HYPNOTICALLY...
HOOVER ELECTED!
HAH! NOW I'VE CAUGHT YEZ MANDUCK AND LOATHAR AND I'M GOING TO GIVE YEZ SOMETHING YOU'RE NOT LIKELY TO FORGET!
CRAK
CRAK
WAK
POW
SOK
THUD

HO BOY, MANDUCK! YOU SURE USE DAT HYPNOTIC GESTURE WISELY FOR GOOD OF MANKIND... NAMELY **US** KIND OF MANKIND!... DAT COP STILL BEATING OLD LADY WIT' KID!
LET'S GO HOME, LOATHAR!
MODEL AGENCY YE OLDE BAG CO.
MANDUCK GESTURES HYPNOTICALLY...
HO!... WE AIN'T **REALLY** GOT HOME BUT MANDUCK GESTURE HYPNO-TICALLY AN' MAKE US T'INK WE LIVE IN FANCY HOUSE!
... NOW TO ENJOY SOME OF THE FINER THINGS IN LIFE!... A BOOK? ... A SYMPHONY? ... **HA... I KNOW...**
MY FIRST RABBIT
MANDUCK GESTURES HYPNOTICALLY...
HO, DAT MAN-DUCK... HIM ALWAYS INTERESTED IN FINER T'INGS IN LIFE... LIKE MAINLY WOMEN!
DZZZZ
OOPS... IS DOOR-BELL!
CHOCALATE COVERED CAVIAR

WESTERN UNION MESSAGE FOR MANDUCK THE MAGICIAN!
- ALSO TRICK OR TREAT!
WESTERN UNION? WHAT MATTER WIT' YOU, KID? YOU MUST NOT COME BY FANCY HIGH-CLASS FRONT ENTRANCE! ALL MESSENGER BOYS IN DIS HIGH-CLASS HOUSE GOT TO COME IN BY SERVANT'S ENTRANCE WAY BACK IN REAR BY GARBAGE CAN RACKS!
PLEASE LEAVE ABANDONED BABIES AT REAR ENTRANCE.
HO WAIT!...ME FORGET MANDUCK NO GESTURE HYPNOTICALLY AT DIS KID SO DIS KID CAN SEE WE SITTIN' IN COUNTY DUMP!
...ME SIGN FOR TELEGRAM 'CAUSE MANDUCK, HIM IS GESTURING HYPNOTICALLY AT HIMSELF IN MIRROR! HIM ON BIG HYPNOTIC JAG!
SHAZAM! SHAZAM!
THAT OL' BLACK MAGIC HAS ME IN A SPIN- THAT OL' BLACK MAGIC THAT I...
5

DASH IT ALL, LOATHAR! HOW MANY TIMES HAVE I TOLD YOU NOT TO INTERRUPT MY HYPNOTIC JAGS! ...AND JUST WHEN SHE WAS INTERESTED IN SEEING MY ETCHINGS!... **WHAT'S THIS? A TELEGRAM?... A MAN WANTS 100 CASES OF SNAKE-OIL? QUICKLY! WE MUST TRAVEL!**
TRAVEL? HOBOY! YOU GONNA GESTURE HYPNOTICALLY? ...YOU GONNA MAKE A CADILLAC? YOU GONNA MAKE AN M.G.? ... A JAGUAR?
C'EST SI BON- SI BON SI BON-
TUXEDO FOR HIRE: WEDDINGS PROMS. FUNERALS BARMITZVAHS EMBALMINGS
MANDUCK GESTURES HYPNOTICALLY...
...NO, LOATHAR! YOU MUST REALIZE, I CAN ONLY GESTURE HYPNCTICALLY TO CREATE ILLUSIONS IN THE MIND!... I **COULD** CREATE THE EFFECT THAT WE ARE RIDING IN A CAR!... HOWEVER WE WOULDN'T ACTUALLY MOVE!... NO, LOATHAR... I THINK WHAT THIS SITUATION CALLS FOR IS A **HORSE!**
HEY! YOU GESTURE HYPNOTICALLY FOR HORSE!... ME NO SEE NO HORSE!... WHY WE NO SEE NO HORSE?
I CASH CLOTHES
WRITE TO: SLOB STATION FLAB N.Y. I, N.Y. —IN NEW JERSEY— BIGELOW 6-7123

ME NO SEE NO HORSE!... NAY! ME NO SEE NUTTIN'!... NAAAAY! HEY! ME FEEL LIKE TAKIN' CANTER DOWN BRIDLE PATH!
PONY RIDE 10¢
TP
N. TURNPIKE J.
HO! NOW ME HUNGRY!... DIS NICE FEED-BAG T'ING YOU GOT FOR ME TO EAT FROM!... YUMMY! NICE FRESH OATS MIXED WIT' OL' DRY HAY-MASH!
LUMPY MATTRESS COMPANY
HA! HERE WE ARE AT HOME OF MAN WHO WANT SNAKE-OIL! YUM! NICE GREEN GRASS FLAVORED WIT' TINY INSECTS!
AH! MANDUCK AND LOATHAR, I PRESUME! COME IN!
DZZ
WELCOME

YOU ARE INTERESTED IN BUYING SNAKE-OIL, SIR?
...WELL... NOT REALLY! THERE'S ANOTHER REASON I BROUGHT YOU HERE! BUT MEANWHILE... JOIN ME IN A CUP OF TEA!... WILL YOU HAVE TWO LUMPS OF SUGAR, LOATHAR?
N-A-A-AY!
BROMO-SELTZER
CARE U.S.A.
CARE U.S.A.
NEDICKS
...ME TAKE WHOLE POT OF LUMPS OF SUGAR ...SPILLUM IN MY FEED-BAG!
YOU SEE, MANDUCK... MY NAME IS LAMONT SHADOWSKEEDEEBOOMBOOM, WEALTHY YOUNG MAN ABOUT TOWN WHO IS IN REALITY THE SHADOW'... SHORT FOR SHADOWSKEEDEEBOOM-BOOM! LONG AGO IN THE ORIENT, I LEARNED A SECRET HYPNOTIC POWER TO CLOUD MEN'S MIND!
SLURP
CRUNCH
SLOBBER
SLOBBER
GULP
LIFE GUARD
6

HOWEVER, I'VE BEEN READING IN THE FUNNY PAPERS THAT YOU TOO HAVE THE SECRET HYPNOTIC POWER TO CLOUD MEN'S MINDS...AND SO IN ORDER TO KEEP MY SECRET EXCLUSIVE, I'LL HAVE TO KNOCK YOU OFF EVEN **THOUGH** THE WEED OF CRIME BEARS BITTER FRUIT!

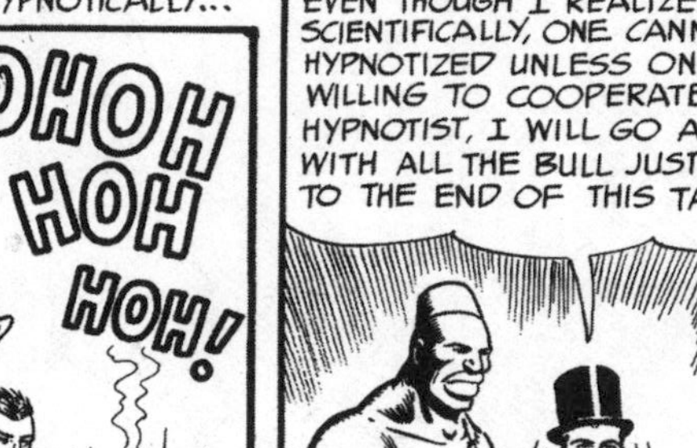
SHADOW GESTURES HYPNOTICALLY...
NYOHOH HOH HOH!
POF

EVEN THOUGH I REALIZE THAT SCIENTIFICALLY, ONE CANNOT BE HYPNOTIZED UNLESS ONE IS WILLING TO COOPERATE WITH HYPNOTIST, I WILL GO ALONG WITH ALL THE BULL JUST TO GET TO THE END OF THIS TALE!

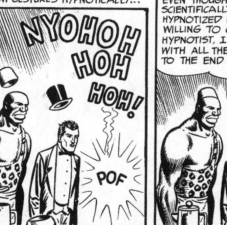

MANDUCK GEST'S. HYP'N'T'C'LY...
POF
POF
SHADOW' GEST'S. HYP'LY...
POF!
MANDUCK GE'S. HY'LY...
POF POF
PIF
SHADOW' G. H....
PAF

MANDUCK G. H...
PURF
LOATHAR G. H...
POFFETY POFF
SHADOW G. H....
PIF PIF PIF
ALL G. H....
PIDIBOFF!
BOOM
7

MY NAME IS NARDA AND I AM WORRIED! YOU SEE, I AM THE GIRL-FRIEND OF MANDUCK THE MAGICIAN! MANDUCK'S BEEN GONE FROM HIS APARTMENT ALL DAY... PROBABLY ON SOME DANGEROUS ADVENTURE! ...AND SO MY NAME IS NARDA AND I AM WORRIED! ...WOULDN'T YOU BE WORRIED IF YOUR NAME WAS NARDA?... WHAT A DOPEY NAME!...WHY COULDN'T IT BE SELMA...OR YVETTE...OR MAYBE SHIRLEY...
...OH! THE DOOR IS OPEN!
MAY IT EVER BE SO HUMBLE THERE'S NO PLACE LIKE THIS!!!
MANDUCK!...LYING CRUMPLED... INSENSIBLE AND DAZED IN THE CORNER...
HOW MANY TIMES I TOLD YOU I WON'T STAND FOR ANY MORE OF THOSE HYPNOTIC JAGS OF YOURS!
ALL DAY I'VE BEEN TRYING TO CALL YOU!... ALL DAY I'VE BEEN RINGING THE CORNER CANDY STORE! ...WHERE'VE YOU BEEN?

WHAT'S THAT?.. WHAT'S THAT YOU'RE MUMBLING ABOUT INTERRUPTIONS AND ETCHINGS?
NEVER MIND, NARDA!... LET'S HAVE A BITE TO EAT WHILE I TELL YOU WHAT HAPPENED!
HMM! NOTHING IN THE ICE-BOX BUT SOME OLD CRUDDY, DRIED OUT HALAVAH!
THRU COURTESY OF BETTY FURNESS
NEVER, NEVER PUT BANANAS IN HERE.
PENICILLIN
...SO MANDUCK GESTURES HYPNOTICALLY...
...YOU SEE... LAMONT SHADOWSKEEDEE-BOOMBOOM, WEALTHY YOUNG MAN ABOUT TOWN, DECIDED TO DESTROY ME SINCE I TOO KNEW THE SECRET HYPNOTIC POWER TO CLOUD MEN'S MINDS! HOWEVER...
STRANGE HOW THIS CAVIAR TASTES LIKE OLD CRUDDY, DRIED-OUT HALAVAH!
THRU COURTESY OF LIBERACE

...WHEN LAMONT CLOUDED MY MIND AND TURNED INTO THE SHADOW, I CLOUDED HIS MIND AND LOATHER AND I TURNED INTO THE SHADOW SO SHADOW CLOUDED OUR MIND AND TURNED INTO LAMONT SO I CLOUDED SHADOW'S MIND WHO TURNED INTO MANDUCK WHO THEN CLOUDED MY MIND AND TURNED ME INTO LOATHAR! I THEN CLOUDED LOATHAR'S MIND AND TURNED HIM INTO MANDUCK WHO THEN CLOUDED MANDUCK AND SHADOW'S MIND AND TURNED THEM INTO LOATHAR... HOWEVER, SHADOW CLOUDED EVERYONE'S MIND AND WE ALL TURNED INTO MANDUCK!
STOP TALKING! YOU'RE FORCING ME OUT OF THE PICTURE!
...THEN ALL THREE MANDUCK'S GESTURED HYPNOTICALLY AND THE WHOLE FURSHLUGGINER MESS BLEW UP IN OUR FACES AND ONLY I AM LEFT!
BUT WHO ARE YOU?... YOU COULD BE EITHER MANDUCK OR SHADOW OR LOATHAR AND AFTER ALL... ONLY ONE OF YOU IS DEAR TO MY HEART AND THAT ONE IS...
TOSSED SALAD
... THE ONE WITH THE MOST LOOT!
...DON'T BE RIDICULOUS, NARDA! THAT HYPNOTIC GESTURING'S A LOT OF FUN, BUT AFTER ALL... IT'S NOT THAT GOOD SO'S I COULDN'T TELL IF I WASN'T MANDUCK!
BIGELOW 6-3211
...BY THE WAY... DID YOU EVER TRY FRESH OATS MIXED WITH DRY HAY MASH? DELICIOUS! HERE...TAKE A CHEW FROM THIS FEED...BAG!
8

ANSWER PAGE

THE REBUS

1. – POTRZEBIE [POT + R + ZEBRA + TIE - RAT]

2. – FELICITATIONS [F (SHORT PRONOUNCIATION OF HALF) ELIC (ELIC IN WONDERLAND) + 'IT (OR HIT) + AT (RHYMES WITH 8) + IONS]

3. – I [WART + ZQUX + ARMPIT + McCARTHY - ZQUX - ARMPIT - WART - McCARTHY + I]

4. – SALAD [TOMATOES + PEPPER + GARLIC + VINEGAR + LETTUCE + OIL + FLIES + SERVING SPOON AND FORK.. TOSS TOGETHER JUST BE-FORE SERVING!]

5. –

6. – BY GEORGE!... WE'RE STILL TRYING TO FIGURE THAT ONE OUT OURSELVES!

HIDDEN ANIMALS

1. – 5 ANIMALS ARE CLEVERLY HIDDEN... A GOAT, A COW, A CHICKEN A PIG AND A DUCK!

2. – MOST OF 115 ANIMALS ARE HIDDEN BEHIND THE SHED. SOME ARE ALSO INSIDE THE SHED!... ALSO, SOME ARE WAY BACK IN BACK OF THE HILL!

THE MEN WHO MAKE MAD

HARVEY KURTZMAN, beagle editor, is married and has two bagles (baby beagles). Drawing from his experience in composing MAD . . . seeing how he's creating laughter, happiness, making living easier in this troubled world, Kurtzman now sees what his ideals, what his purpose, his goal should be. Kurtzman now understands what is the most precious thing in life. These ideals, this purpose, this goal, this precious thing in life is . . . mainly . . . money.

BILL ELDER is a complete idiot. He is kept locked in a steel cage in Englewood, N. J., where once a month his hairy, claw-like hand is seen to emerge through a trap in the door with a set of drawings. Then, clutching a slab of raw beef (Elder gets paid in raw beef), the hand withdraws into the darkness, not to be seen again until the next month.

JACK DAVIS is a colorful character from the deep South. On a clear summer day, Jack can be seen charging from the elevator, shrieking the rebel yell down the hall to the comic-book office, where he demolishes the door pane with his percussion rifle, spears his pay check with his needle bayonet, and dashes away to buy Confederate money.

WALLACE WOOD, as well as being a fine comic cartoonist, is one of the leading science-fiction cartoonists in the U. S. One is amazed . . . often puzzled . . . at the authentic quality and detail of Wood's drawings of machines from outer space. And even more baffling is the third eye one occasionally sees, concealed as it is in a furrow of Wood's forehead.

Presenting

THE MAD READER

"A book you will want to read and treasure as a keepsake . . . "*

Comprehensive, authoritative, filling an essential need, The MAD Reader has brought doubt and wild confusion into the lives of thousands of formerly sane and well-adjusted readers. Over half a million satisfied buyers have this to say about The MAD Reader:

B-L-E-C-H-H-H!

Obtain your copy today

****(Afterwards it can be used for wrapping fish.)***

A Potrzebie Book Published by

ibooks, inc.
24 West 25th Street 11th Fl.
New York

INSIDE
MAD
With a Backword by
STAN FREBERG
MAD
THINK

From ibooks—

The *MAD* Reader
MAD Strikes Back!
Inside *MAD*
Utterly *MAD*
The Brothers *MAD*